INSIDE GIRL

inside girl

Also by J. Minter:

the insiders
pass it on
take it off
break every rule
hold on tight
girls we love

INSIDE GIRL

a novel by J. MINTER
author of the insiders

BLOOMSBURY

BLOOMSBURY

Copyright © 2007 by J. Minter
and 17th Street Productions, an Alloy company

Published by Bloomsbury U.S.A. Children's Books
175 Fifth Avenue, New York, NY 10010
Distributed to the trade by Holtzbrinck Publishers

Library of Congress Cataloging-in-Publication Data
Minter, J.
Inside girl : a novel / by J. Minter. — 1st U.S. ed.
p.   cm.
Summary: Flan Flood, younger sister of the handsome and popular Patch, just wants to fit in when she starts high school in New York City, but her crazy friends Liesel, Sara-Beth, and Philippa make it anything but easy for her.
ISBN-13: 978-1-59990-086-5 • ISBN-10: 1-59990-086-6
[1. Friendship—Fiction. 2. Popularity—Fiction. 3. High schools—Fiction.
4. Schools—Fiction. 5. Dating (Social customs)—Fiction.
6. New York (N.Y.)—Fiction.] I. Title.
PZ7.S3872Imm 2007   [Fic]—dc22   2006028190

ALLOYENTERTAINMENT   Produced by Alloy Entertainment
                      151 West 26th Street, New York, NY 10001

First U.S. Edition 2007
Printed in the U.S.A. by Quebecor World Fairfield
10 9 8 7 6 5 4 3 2

for **CKS**

Chapter 1

Our yellow Mercedes convertible turned a corner onto Perry Street, and I breathed a sigh of relief. I'd spent the whole long summer in boring Connecticut, but now, thank God, I was back in the city again.

And, more important, I was free.

My brother, Patch, was driving, and our sister, Feb, was supposedly in the city somewhere, but our parents were staying in Connecticut for a couple more weeks, to go to a horse show and go yachting and stuff while the weather was still nice. After that they might go on to Marrakech, to see some sultan's palace or something. It used to make me nervous when they went traveling for weeks without us, but I was used to it by now. This time, I was even glad they were going to be away for a little while. As much as I love them, they're so scatterbrained and wrapped up in their own lives that they drive me kind of nuts sometimes.

1

Besides, I was fourteen years old and about to start my first year of high school. I figured I was old enough to take care of myself. After all, Patch and Feb had started taking care of themselves as freshmen, and look how they turned out.

"Looks like some of your friends are here to welcome you home, Flan," Patch said as he turned off the engine and double-parked in front of our town house.

The three girls I'd been hoping to avoid most were standing right there on the sidewalk staring at us: Angelica, Camille, and Beverly. They weren't in school uniforms, but they might as well have been. Beverly and Camille were both wearing those footless leggings that just came back in style, and all three of them had on these gauzy, faux-vintage tank tops in pastel colors. We'd all gone to this private girls' school on the East Side together from the time we were little kids—until now. I wasn't going back to Miss Mallard's Day this year. But of course they didn't know that yet.

"Flan! It's so good to see you!" they cried, rushing over to me. After a tornado of air-kisses, I stepped back, leaned against the car, and counted the milliseconds before the questions started.

"So," said Camille, sneaking a look at Patch, who was unloading our bags from the trunk. "We're *dying*

2

to know how your summer has been! Where did you go? What did you do? Who did you meet?"

I shrugged. "I dunno. Like I said in May, I was just out at our place in Old Greenwich all summer."

"But what about your brother and sister? What parties did they take you to?" pressed Angelica. She sat down on the steps to our house, like she was settling in for a long conversation.

"I didn't really go to any parties. Mostly I just rode my bike and went swimming and stuff. On the Fourth, I watched the fireworks from my parents' sailboat. Seriously." Actually, I had gone to a few parties out on the beach with Feb—there was this one really wild one where some guys from the house next to ours roasted a goat—but I wasn't about to tell them that. One little story and they'd be pumping me for details for the next fifteen minutes. And I wasn't in the mood to recap my entire summer just then.

"Well, what about Patch?" Beverly whispered. An air conditioner dripped onto her head, but she didn't seem to notice. "Did he have a good summer? Is he . . . seeing anyone?"

"I don't know," I said in a normal tone of voice, right as Patch walked by us carrying a couple of suitcases. "Why don't you just ask him yourself?"

Angelica, Camille, and Beverly all just stared at me

like I'd killed Santa Claus. And that right there is exactly the reason I wasn't going back to Miss Mallard's Day.

You've probably heard of the Floods: February and Patch, my older sister and brother. Their parties, their celebrity friends, their VIP passes. Both of them are gorgeous (not to brag, but good looks run in our family), and by the time they were my age, they were both as popular as any Manhattan private school teenager can possibly be—which, believe me, is pretty popular.

You might think that having them as siblings would be the coolest thing ever, and in some ways you'd be right: there's a reason everybody likes them so much. But let me tell you firsthand, there's nothing as uncool as having your friends more interested in your siblings than in you. Sure, I could have a party at a cool club like Lotus, like I had for my birthday at the beginning of the summer. It hadn't made any difference: by July the only friend who even bothered to call me was my old pal Liv, and she just wanted to grill me on what was going on with Patch, who she—like most all the girls I know—is so totally obsessed with that she's fooled herself into thinking it's love.

"So," said Camille, to fill up the shocked silence still hanging in the air. "Did you hear about the new uniform rule? Ramona Wood's mother is on the committee, and she said they voted to make the skirt two inches shorter."

"Finally," said Angelica. "Thank God we don't have to start high school looking like nuns."

"Listen, guys," I said, because now seemed as good a time as any. "I've got something to tell you. I'm not going to Miss Mallard's this year."

"*What?!*" all three of them cried at once.

"I got into Stuyvesant. I would have told you in the spring, but I wasn't sure what I was going to do, and Stuyvesant held a place for me. So I'm doing it. I'm going to public school."

The girls all looked confused and almost scared, like I'd just told them I was committing myself to a mental institution.

"But Flan, you're a Flood," Camille breathed. I could tell she was upset, because even though a cute guy in Diesel jeans came out of a town house right across the street from us, she didn't take her eyes off me for a second.

"So?"

"Your sister's a legend at Miss Mallard's. Your brother was voted hottest private school boy. You're *legacy* cool. Why would you give that up? For a *public* school?"

I shook my head. "Listen, if you guys don't understand it already, I don't think I can explain it to you."

And with that, I walked into the house. The truth is, I'd been prepping for that moment for the past two months and now that it had happened, I was deliriously happy and almost kind of in shock. I'd done it! The first true speech uttered by the new Flan!

So I was glad to get away from those three. But once I was inside the town house, it seemed awfully big and empty all of a sudden.

"Feb?" I yelled, dropping my bags in the foyer. I stepped out into the living room. "Anybody home?"

My older sister, February, had supposedly been living in the attic for most of the summer, but except for a lipstick-stained wineglass on the coffee table that looked like it had been there for weeks, I didn't see signs of her anywhere. Patch tossed his duffel down next to mine, then glanced around aimlessly.

"I think I'll go out for a sandwich," he said, trying to stifle a yawn. "You gonna be all right here by yourself?"

"Sure," I said—I kind of didn't want to be by myself, but it wasn't like I'd never been home alone before. "I'll be fine."

"Okay, well, call me if you need anything. I'll be back."

When Patch left, he didn't even bother closing the door all the way behind him. And the thing about Patch is that going out for a sandwich could equal being gone for an hour or a day or a week. He could go out for a sandwich and end up on a mountaintop in Nepal or surfing off the coast of Australia. Which is why I didn't bother to ask him to bring me back a coffee yogurt.

After I locked the door and put the chain on for good measure, I glanced around. Our house is really nice—three floors if you count the attic, four if you count the basement—and the living room is one of the best places in it. It always cheers me up to sit in there. Mom and Dad aren't huge art collectors, but a few years ago they went to Florence and found this great Italian artist who does all these sort-of-Cubist-but-not-really ink-on-paper drawings. They bought the whole show and shipped it home and now his pictures are all over our walls: colorful little shapes and noodly lines. Then they have this great supermodern sofa, made of soft leather and sort of shaped like a Nike swoosh, but unlike a lot of designer furniture it's really comfortable, and it's got all these llama-fur afghans on it that they found in Peru a few years ago. There's a glass coffee table, usually covered with remotes for the TV and all the different VCRs and CD and DVD players, not to mention some video game controllers. Across from that is our entertainment system. Through the door at the far end of the room is our kitchen, which is usually bright and sparkly clean. Right now, though, the whole house looked dark and unused and somehow a lot less friendly than I remembered.

What was I going to do for the rest of the afternoon? I could curl up on the couch and watch my new DVD of *Some Like It Hot*, but I'd already binged on old movies back in Connecticut, and it seemed pretty dumb to keep on doing that now that I was back in New York. I should be doing something fun, something wild and independent, something grown-up. Or at least I shouldn't just be standing around. Maybe I should have gone out for a sandwich with Patch and seen where that led me.

Before I could even step away from the door, though, the bell rang urgently, three times in a row. I figured it was Patch, just having forgotten his money or what his mission was or whatever, and so I opened it without even looking through the peephole. Now that he was back, maybe he'd take me with him. Sure, I'd be tagging along, but so what? I didn't feel like being alone in this big dark house. When I opened the door, though, I saw it wasn't my brother at all.

Her tiny face was almost hidden behind a huge pair of sunglasses with black, round frames that reminded me of Mickey Mouse ears, and even though it was sweltering outside, she was bundled up in a gray mink coat that was about ten sizes too big for her. She'd put on a weird old lady wig, all white and puffy. Underneath it, strands of her short dark hair were sticking out, all hot and squashed looking. And before I could say anything, she'd shoved me back inside and locked the door behind her.

Chapter 2

ara-Beth Benny," I gasped. "What are you doing here?"

Sara-Beth threw her mink coat on the floor and kicked it away from her. Beneath it she had on a vintage flapper dress that looked like it was made entirely of spangles and ostrich feathers, like something Catherine Zeta-Jones would wear in *Chicago*. That's Sara-Beth for you: even when she's wearing her own clothes, she looks like she's in costume.

"Oh, Flan, I knew you'd see through my disguise. That's why you're such a true friend. You know the real me even better than I know the real me."

I shook my head. I doubted I was the only one who'd recognized her. Tourists had probably been following her around the West Village and snapping pictures of her all afternoon. In case you don't know, Sara-Beth Benny is one of the most famous seventeen-year-olds around. After she grew up on national television as the most adorable star of *Mike's Princesses*, she started getting parts in all kinds of really cool movies—like this really creepy thriller called *Blennophobia*, and a remake of this French New Wave movie. She even tried her hand at comedy in *The Seventeen-Year-Old Virgin*. I've always preferred old movies, myself, but I think Sara-Beth Benny's a really good actress, and I'd say that even if we weren't friends. When her eyes get all big and her lower lip starts quivering, she can make you believe whatever she wants.

"But wait. I still don't know what you're doing here. Aren't you supposed to be filming a movie in Gdansk or something?" Sara-Beth definitely had a decent excuse for not calling me all summer, since she'd been halfway around the world for the last couple months.

"Oh, Ric Roderickson, that idiotic director—he makes me so furious, I can't even talk about it. The catering people couldn't get my uva-ursi, so of course my face starts swelling up like a balloon. So what does he do? Does he find me an acupuncturist? No. He cut two of my scenes. And I had to come home early to a very toxic apartment."

"But wait, how would an acupuncturist—"

"Well, that was a separate thing." She threw herself down onto the couch with a sigh. "Oh, Flan, I just can't talk about it anymore. It's just so good to be home, with my real friends. I couldn't talk to those people on the set anyway. The guys were all so strange and hyper, and the girls were all prima donnas. Do you have any clothespins? Well, do you?"

Sara-Beth tossed the old lady wig behind the couch and raked her fingers through her short hair. She's so tiny and nervous that she sometimes reminds me of a Chihuahua. The first time I met her, at a sweet sixteen party for our friend Liesel Reid, we were in line for the bathroom, and I thought she was jumpy just because she really had to go. But it turned out that's just the way she always is.

"I don't know." I glanced around. I couldn't imagine anyone in our family buying clothespins, and I didn't want to know what weird holistic remedy Sara-Beth needed them for.

"Well, that's all right, it can wait." And all of a sudden she was standing up again, and she rushed over to me and took both of my hands in hers. She looked intently into my face. "How are you, Flan? I mean, really? Have you missed me?"

I stared at the two tiny Flans reflected in her enormous eyes. The Flans looked back, a little nervously.

"Sure. Of course. I just got back from Connecticut, though, so I haven't really—"

"Oh, good. Because I've missed you too. When I was in Gdansk, surrounded by all those . . . energy vampires, I kept thinking about that wonderful sleepover you threw for me back in May, and just how simple you are."

"Well, thanks."

I wasn't sure how I felt about being called simple, but like I said, Sara-Beth is very convincing, and I could tell her heart was in the right place. Besides, it had been fun having her over for that sleepover, even if she did refuse to eat anything but the bag of rice crisps she'd brought for herself. It had also been a little weird when the doorbell rang and she freaked out and hid under the bed. It was just one of Feb's friends, but it took almost an hour to convince Sara-Beth that it wasn't the paparazzi.

"Which is why I feel like I can ask you for a favor. It's not anything too big, and I know you'll understand."

"Of course," I heard myself say. "I'd love to help you, Sara-Beth."

"Oh, good! Oh, fabulous!" Sara-Beth sighed with relief and hugged me. I could feel her bony elbows pressing into my back before she finally let go. "Wonderful. Just let me get my bags."

"Bags? But—"

"You see, as I just mentioned about half a dozen times, my apartment is *toxic*. Everything's so . . . sharp, and cold, and empty, and metallic. And it's lonely there." It was true: the one time I'd visited, I'd been amazed at how little stuff she had. Her apartment was basically four thousand square feet that contained a Mies van der Rohe chair, a tube of lip gloss, a bottle of Dom Pérignon, and about eight closets full of clothes.

"And I can't go stay with David again, not even if he begs me to." Sara-Beth gazed dreamily off into the distance. "Sweet, gentle David. He had to leave Gdansk even earlier than I did. He must be heartbroken, being without me for so long. I'd love to be with him, I really would, but I have to think of his folks. That's a lot to ask of your future in-laws, you know."

"Right," I said. David is a friend of my brother's, and at one point, Sara-Beth lived with his family for about six months. His parents are psychiatrists, so I guess they were fascinated by Sara-Beth, since she'd always been a celebrity and had never really had a chance to just be a kid. They even wrote an article on her for the *New York Times* magazine's health column, called "Beyond Help? A Case Study of America's Favorite Starlet."

"I'm trying to get a nice little place near where Liesel lives on the Upper East Side, in this charming building with all this . . . wood, you know, and views of the park. I need to be around nature. It's just the way I am. But this ridiculous board has to approve me first. They think they're so exclusive, just because the building used to be Shakespeare's birthplace or the Australian embassy or something—it's all very historical. It makes me crazy. Flan . . ." And now she gripped my wrists again in the steely bones of her hands and her eyes grew a few degrees bigger and started to well up. "Flan, could I spend the night? I just need some time for girl talk."

I blinked. "I mean—I have school tomorrow, but I guess that—"

"Oh, thank you, thank you, thank you! You have no idea how much this means to me. This will be so much fun. I can help you get ready for your first day!"

Shaking my head and smiling, I walked back toward the kitchen and poured myself a glass of water from one of the bottles in the fridge. It was great to see SBB again—she's really funny and sweet, on top of being glamorous—and I was glad I wasn't alone in the apartment anymore. I pictured us staying up late, doing each other's hair and talking about how totally gross Gdansk can be in August. The whole situation was a little funny, though. After all, my first day at a normal high school was tomorrow, and now there was a movie star staying at my house who even on her very best days had only a very loose grip on reality.

That night, while I was loading up my backpack with stuff for school—pens, paper, a binder—Sara-Beth Benny lay on my bed, turning her wig over in her hands and offering me advice about high school.

"The most important thing is, don't show them you're afraid," she said. "Also, try to dress older than you are. You're lucky that you're tall and stuff, but maybe you should put some extra socks in your bra, just in case."

I zipped up my bag. "Sara-Beth?"

"Hmm?"

"No offense or anything, but did you ever actually *go* to high school?"

"Sure. In some of the later seasons I did. That's how I know about the socks. Because there was this one episode when I wore these Tupperware containers under my shirt—"

"No, not on *Mike's Princesses*." I tucked a graphing calculator into the front pocket of my bag. "Did you ever go to high school in real life?"

Sara-Beth yawned. "Well, life imitates art, you know?"

"That makes sense, I guess." I picked up my backpack and set it on a chair, then turned toward my closet. "Okay, now I just need to figure out what to wear."

"This is my favorite part!" Sara-Beth leaped up. "I love going through your closet."

"You do?"

"Sure. The last time I stayed over, I couldn't sleep, so I tried on all your clothes and pretended I was you. You've got some nice stuff in there. And you don't even have a stylist!"

"Wait, you what?"

She beamed. "Method acting."

So Sara-Beth and I went through my closet. I tried on half a dozen outfits before we found one that satisfied both of us. I was kind of confused about what would be right, since I'd always had uniforms for school at Miss Mallard's Day. I knew what to wear to a gallery show, a record release party, a club, and the opening of a new tapas restaurant, but somehow the haute couture for second-period English class seemed less obvious. Basically, I just wanted something that would look cute but wouldn't draw too much attention to me if it wasn't quite right.

Sara-Beth, on the other hand, kept steering me toward the flashiest, strangest stuff she could find in the depths of my closet. She made me put on a grass-green Miu Miu dress I'd bought to wear to my cousin's wedding, a canary-yellow cashmere sweater that I've had since fifth grade, and a pair of moon boots, among other things. Then she started talking about how we should go uptown and raid her wardrobe, since she was on *People*'s best-dressed list two years in a row, but as much as I'd like to wear some of her dresses, they were way too fancy and probably all too small for me anyway. So instead I finally settled on this really cute vintage crocheted top of mine, which sort of looks hippie-ish but in a clean way, and a pair of these stretch denim jeans that work really well with heels.

A little bit later, I changed into my pajamas and we lay on the floor looking at magazines. It was nice, just hanging out with her, eating her rice crisps and drinking mineral water. If I didn't pay too much attention to her perfect skin or the fashion-spread pictures of her in the magazines I was reading, I could almost forget she was a movie star. And more important, she could too.

I mean, if I thought growing up in my house was weird, how weird must it have been for Sara-Beth, growing up on the set of a hit TV show? If I could make her feel a little more normal by letting her crash in my room, well, that's what friends are for. Besides, having her around took my mind off my own worries. Sometimes when I'm freaking out, it's easier for me to think about someone else's problems instead of my own. And Sara-Beth definitely had her own set of problems.

"I'm glad you came to visit," I told her, reaching for a rice crisp. "You know, I'll be at school tomorrow, but if you want to hang out here for a while and have a friend over for lunch or something, you totally should. I don't want you to be sitting in your apartment, feeling lonely all day."

"Oh, but Flan, I couldn't do that." Sara-Beth's eyes got wide, just like in the mascara ads. "If the paparazzi find out where I am, they'll swarm."

"How would they find out? If you just call one of your friends—"

"You can't trust anyone in this business." Sara-Beth crunched a rice crisp angrily. "I know girls who would sell me out to the tabloids for one positive article and a handful of diet pills. They're that vicious."

"That's terrible." It really was. Even if my friends at

Miss Mallard's used me sometimes, for concert tickets or invitations, at least they never turned on me like
that. What else could I say?

"And if that does happen, I can say good-bye to
that beautiful apartment on the East Side."

"How come?"

Sara-Beth sighed. "The board doesn't want a
bunch of crazy stalker paparazzi lurking outside their
building all the time. If they see I'm always in the
tabloids, they won't want me living there. And then
I'll be homeless." Her lower lip stuck out. "I don't
know where I'd go, or what I'd do. I'll have to buy a
car and park outside your house and just live there
forever. Maybe you could bring me out some water
from time to time."

"I can't believe that."

"But it's true. It can be a mean world out there.
You're lucky you haven't seen it yet."

"Is there anything I can do to help?"

"Well, actually, I was meaning to ask you something."

"Sure, go ahead."

"Please tell me if you don't have time, but I was
wondering—okay, so the co-op board says that I can
submit a peer recommendation along with my application. You know, someone who knows what it's like to

live with me. I was just thinking that maybe, if it wasn't too, too, too much trouble—"

"Of course, Sara-Beth! I'd be happy to."

"Oh, thank you so much. You don't know how much this means to me. You're the only one who knows what I'm really like, underneath." Sara-Beth folded back the cover of her magazine, then looked over at me, suddenly all serious. "That's what I like about you, Flan. You're not my friend because I'm beautiful, or famous, or because of what I could do for you. You're my friend because—because of who I really am." Sara-Beth sniffled, and all her little bones trembled. She reminded me of a skinny kitten left out in the cold. "I know I can trust you."

"Of course. I'm glad I can help you get the apartment. And I won't tell anyone that you're staying here either. I promise."

"Wonderful. A secret!" She smiled. "Oh, this is going to be *cr-azy* fun!"

And then—and I'm being totally serious—SBB meowed at me and sort of wriggled around and then threw herself on my bed and kicked up her feet.

The next morning, when my alarm clock went off, I felt like I was still dreaming. Was it possible that the time had really come? My first day at Stuyvesant?

After twisting and turning in front of the mirror for about twenty minutes, I finally did my hair up in a messy bun, put on some watermelon-flavored lip gloss, and gave myself a final once-over. I looked good, I thought: the heels I'd picked really dressed up my jeans, and my skin, which is normally super pale, actually had some color to it since I'd spent all summer biking and hanging out down by the shore. And at this point, there was nothing else I could do to make myself look cooler or older. So I grabbed my backpack and went downstairs. SBB was still asleep in one of the bedrooms upstairs—I'm not even sure which one.

When I went down to the kitchen to drink a quick

glass of orange juice before school, I noticed something I hadn't seen before: a message on the answering machine. I pushed the button and it played into the room.

"Hey, Patch? Flan? It's Feb. So, it's Saturday night, and I'm just calling to say I might be gone for a few days. This friend of mine's shooting a music video in this abandoned warehouse in Brooklyn and I'm going to chill out there for a while. Don't tell Mom and Dad. Obviously. I hope everything's cool. Keep the peace while I'm gone."

I sighed and walked out the door. I wondered if Feb ever felt nervous or awkward or uncool. Probably not.

Unlike Miss Mallard's, which is a long cab ride away, Stuyvesant is actually within walking distance of my house. So I took my time on the walk over. I love my neighborhood in the morning. Everything looks so fresh and pretty. Sometime either late at night or really early, somebody must hose down all the sidewalks, because they're always wet and sparkly in the morning sun, and even though I live right in the middle of New York City, the air smells like window-box flowers and tree leaves instead of garbage and taxi exhaust. As I walked down the street, I saw store owners pulling up the metal gates in the fronts of their stores and turning on the lights in the display cases, and I started to feel a little happier for some reason, like maybe today wasn't such an awfully big deal after all.

As soon as I started walking down Chambers Street, though, I started to feel super anxious. Stuyvesant takes up a whole big building—ten floors, with escalators—and I could see it looming up from more than a block away. The doors to the building hadn't opened yet, but already there were a million kids milling around on the sidewalk outside, and even more coming down the street or across the Tribeca Bridge. I didn't know any of them.

It couldn't have been more different from Miss Mallard's Day, where everybody wore a uniform and knew everybody else. Here all the students were divided up into cliques that couldn't have been crazier or more different from one another. There were guys all thugged out in baggy jeans and sports jerseys, kids with white faces and black lips who looked like they were auditioning for a Tim Burton movie, girls in professional-looking skirts and blouses who could have been in law school, plus raver types in bright colors and kids in dark baggy T-shirts with anime characters and computer jargon printed on them. My outfit had seemed so cool back at my house, but now I wasn't so sure. I felt really out of place—and young looking. Sara-Beth was right: everyone in high school seemed like they were trying to look as much older as possible. Some of the guys even had beards.

I didn't know what to do, so I just sort of wandered through the crowd like I was looking for someone I knew, which I kind of was, in a way. I passed a really chesty girl in a glittery BOYS LIE T-shirt and tight short-shorts, a punked-out kid who had so many piercings he looked like he'd fallen asleep with his head down on a sewing machine, and a really cute guy in a polo shirt who looked old enough to be in a frat before I finally gave up and sat down on the sidewalk with my back against the wall, all by myself. Even then I felt like just a speck in the crowd.

It was weird: I'd been to a million parties where the other kids were older, but everyone always recognized me. I was usually with my sister or my brother or my ex-boyfriend, Jonathan, but even when I was alone, I was always Flan Flood, and people knew that. I never just blended in—I was always getting noticed and singled out, interrogated, practically, by gossipmongers and hangers-on. At the time I hated it, but sitting there on the sidewalk outside the high school, I started to think that maybe Angelica and Camille and the other girls from my old school were right—maybe I was giving up something pretty special by leaving

Miss Mallard's Day. Maybe it wasn't such a great idea to strike off on my own like this. Maybe I'd found my true self—and she was a wallflower.

Just when I was feeling about ready to cry, though, I saw them: two other girls who looked just as lost as I did. They were both kind of tall, like me. One of them had wavy light brown hair pulled back in a ponytail, and an awesome skirt made out of men's ties stitched together lengthwise. The other one was sort of preppy, with long blond hair that she kept flipping back over her shoulders while she looked around the crowd. They were whispering to each other and their mouths were just barely moving, as if they were afraid they'd get in trouble if anyone figured out what they were saying.

I wanted to go talk to them, but for a minute I couldn't make myself get up from the spot I'd claimed on the sidewalk. What if I went over and said hi, and they thought I was some desperate loser and totally blew me off? I'd feel so lame. But then again, the only way to stop *being* a desperate loser was to make some friends. High school was supposed to be my big opportunity to meet new people, right? So I stood up, literally dusted myself off, and made my feet move in their direction.

I knew right away I'd made the right decision, because when they saw me, they both looked over with really friendly, relieved-looking smiles.

"Hi," said the girl in the tie skirt, smiling at me. She had really pretty little teeth, and now that I was closer I could see she was wearing a shirt with flowers embroidered all over it in different colors of ribbon. "I'm Meredith."

"I'm Flan. Flan Flood." I figured I might as well get it out of the way—but when I said "Flood," they didn't react at all. They just kept smiling at me in the same relieved, friendly way. So they hadn't heard of Patch and Feb? It was a thrill and sort of unsettling at the same time—like walking around on Halloween in a mask and discovering that people really can't tell who you are. "I really like your skirt," I added, to cover my confusion. "Did you make it?"

"Oh, no. My grandma did." Meredith gave her skirt a little twirl. "Isn't it great? She designs clothes. She has a little shop in Soho—my mom works there too."

"That's so awesome." I grinned, but inside I panicked a little. What would I say if they asked me what my parents did for a living? "They like to travel, and sometimes my dad buys cars or boats if he's bored"? If I wanted to seem normal, that was not the best way to start out.

"I'm Judith," said the other girl. She talked like she'd had voice lessons or something, and she kept flipping her long blond hair over her shoulders, but she seemed nice and I decided to like her anyway. "Are you new here too?"

"Yeah, this is my first day."

Meredith pushed her hair off her shoulders. "Well, except for orientation, of course, but I guess that didn't really count."

"Orientation? What?" I felt a sinking feeling in my stomach, like when you find out there's going to be a test you haven't studied for.

Meredith and Judith exchanged a glance.

"I thought we hadn't seen her before," said Meredith.

"I just got back from Connecticut yesterday," I said.

"Well, don't worry about it," said Meredith, squeezing my arm. "It was mostly just a tour anyway. And we made ugly friendship bracelets." She and Judith held up their wrists, and I looked. They really were the ugliest friendship bracelets I'd ever seen. "Judith and I can show you around the building and stuff."

"Really?"

"Of course," said Judith. "I've got a terrific memory for these things."

We took out our schedules and figured out that we were in most of the same classes, except Meredith had gotten into honors English, which seemed to irritate Judith a little, since, as she pointed out, she was *normally* the better student. We all sat together in the back of the auditorium for the first-day assembly, and I found out all about the two of them.

Apparently, they'd gone to an all-girls private school on the West Side all through elementary school and junior high, and they'd been best friends since either of them could remember. Meredith was really into arts and crafts, and from what she said it sounded like she'd wind up working in her mom and grandma's clothing store before too long, unless she decided she liked painting or photography better. Judith was more into getting good grades, especially in math, and she told me twice that she'd been the valedictorian of their eighth-grade class. Her father was a personal injury lawyer—"You've probably seen his ads on the subway," she said.

"Oh, yeah," I said. The last time I'd been down in the subway was this one night when Feb took me out with her friends and we got stranded down near Battery Park at two in the morning with no cabs anywhere in sight. Feb and I had walked down into the subway station, taken one look at the dripping ceilings of doom and the sketchy fat drunk guy passed out on a bench, and called a car service.

I didn't pay much attention during the assembly, since Meredith and Judith and I were talking the whole time, but I did find out that in the afternoon we were supposed to have quick meetings in all of our classes so the teachers could tell us what books to buy and what the first assignment would be. After representatives from all the different clubs and sports teams and study groups got up and talked about themselves, they finally let us take a break—to go have some lunch in the cafeteria.

"So, Flan, we've been talking about ourselves forever," said Judith as we sat down to eat by one of the windows. The cafeteria at Stuyvesant is beautiful, and you can see right out to the Hudson River. It's so different from the stuffy old tearoom where we ate lunch at Miss Mallard's; instead, we were on the first floor, and we could see ladies walking past the windows with their little dogs, and beyond them were boats and ferries and maybe even the *QE2* out there in the Hudson River. "What about you? Where did you go to school before? What's your story?"

"Oh, there's nothing much to tell about me." I turned a fork around in my spinach fettuccine. "I went to this place called Miss Mallard's Day. It was all girls too."

Judith took a bite of her yogurt. "I can't believe

how some girls our age have already had a bunch of boyfriends. I feel like I've barely seen a boy since kindergarten."

"Really," I said, thinking of the hot older boys milling around at my brother's parties.

"Speaking of which," whispered Meredith, hunching over and pointing across the room to the soda machines.

Judith and I both turned around to look. And there he was: tousled dirty-blond hair, squinty blue-gray eyes, and a gentle smile that showed his slightly chipped front tooth. He wore a ripped All-American Rejects T-shirt and long denim shorts, and he walked so gracefully I could tell he'd be great at slow dancing.

"Who's that?" I whispered back.

"Bennett Keating." Meredith giggled. "He's the second-cutest boy in tenth grade!"

I watched him walk over to a table of other guys. "Who's the first?"

"Well, according to Judith it's this guy named Eric. But I hear he's really stuck-up. You know, always talking about his penthouse apartment . . ."

". . . and all the celebrities he knows . . ."

". . . and all the exclusive parties he gets invited to," Meredith finished.

Judith rolled her eyes and settled them on a pigeon

outside. "I mean, who cares about that stuff anyway? It's so shallow, you know? That doesn't make you cool. Nobody cares, Eric. Nobody." She chomped down on an apple slice like the case was closed.

"Yeah," I said. I'd started to feel really comfortable around them, but all of a sudden I just wanted to hide. I pretended to admire the view out the window and tried not to think about Sara-Beth Benny, who was at that moment probably practicing her Oscar speech in front of my mirror. I went on. "I'd rather people like me . . . just for myself, you know?" I barely managed a weak smile.

Chapter 5

After school, I walked with Meredith and Judith over to the subway, which they were taking back to their apartments uptown. Meredith was telling us about how she saw Bennett Keating try to fill his Nalgene bottle at the water fountain, only to get totally drenched, and I was laughing so hard that I started to follow them down the stairs into the subway station before I even realized what I was doing.

"Oh, hey, I guess I should say good-bye here," I said, stepping aside so a woman carrying a stroller could walk past me.

"You're not taking the subway home?" Judith asked, flipping her hair.

"No, I only live a few blocks away from school. It's a nice walk, actually."

"Oh, wow, that's so cool," said Meredith. "I don't think I met anyone else at orientation who lives so close."

"What's it like, living in the Village?" asked Judith. "Are there a lot of rich artists and stuff?"

"Yeah, a few," I said, thinking of Mickey Pardo, one of Patch's friends, whose father is this famous sculptor. A whole team of kids in soccer uniforms came barreling down the stairs around us, and I held on to the banister. "Wait, I'll follow you down. We can talk while you're waiting for the train."

Meredith, Judith, and I went down into the subway station. Somehow, subway stations always seem kind of gross and drippy, even when it's not raining outside, and this one was no exception. There were puddles on the concrete, stalactites of peeling paint coming down from the ceiling, and a weird odor that reminded me of the way our basement at the summerhouse smells after a thunderstorm. Ugh. I knew I liked Meredith and Judith a lot, though, because hanging out with them made it worth it to be down there. I didn't have a MetroCard, but Meredith swiped us both through on hers so I could come onto the platform with them.

The three of us walked down to a little newsstand inside the station where they sold candy and magazines. Meredith bought a roll of Lifesavers while Judith picked up a copy of *People* and started leafing through it.

"We'll have to hang out at your place sometime," she said.

"That would be nice," I said. "Actually, if you're not doing anything tomorrow—" I was about to invite them over right then and there, but just as I opened my mouth, I glanced down at a copy of *Us Weekly* sitting on the newsstand shelf.

On its cover, Sara-Beth Benny was trying to get out of a taxi, but you could tell she was totally surrounded by paparazzi. Her collar was up to hide her face, and she had on the big dark glasses she'd been wearing the day before. She was holding up one hand like she was trying to shield herself from the photographer's flash. The headline read, "Does She Eat at All?" It was a good thing I saw it when I did, because it occurred to me that it was highly likely that Sara-Beth would still be camped out at my house—and she probably wouldn't like two strangers shrieking and asking for autographs when they saw her there. "Oh, I just remembered, they're renovating the cupboards in our kitchen, and my mom made me promise not to have people over until they're finished."

Meredith and Judith exchanged a look—or maybe I imagined it. But for just a second, it seemed like they didn't quite believe me. It was gone before I could be sure I'd seen it, though. I felt awkward, so I looked the other way down the long subway platform, at a guy with an acoustic guitar who was playing at the other end, until Judith finally said, "We can totally wait until after it's finished. No problem."

"Thanks," I said. "I'm so glad I met you guys today."

"Me too," Meredith said. "Ooh! Maybe we should meet here tomorrow morning, before school? That way we can walk in together."

Judith nodded. "We got here at about quarter to eight today, so it should be around then tomorrow too."

"That sounds great," I said. "Meet up at the top of the steps?"

"Awesome."

Their train pulled into the station then, and we hugged good-bye. As it clanked away, I felt like I should be waving a handkerchief or something like they do in old movies. But fortunately, it wasn't like they were leaving on a voyage to the farthest ends of the earth. I was seeing them tomorrow—I even knew when.

As I left the subway, I felt pretty good. I'd survived my first day and I'd even made two friends. Or at least I hoped I had. There was still the possibility that they would decide I was a snob when they got to know me better and found out about all the celebrities I'd met and parties I'd been to, but I was trying not to think too hard about that. With any luck, I'd begun to hope, they'd know the real me before they found out about all that stuff anyway.

Chapter 6

It was so quiet back at my house that I thought Sara-Beth had probably gone back to her toxic apartment, and I started kicking myself for having made up that stupid lie about the kitchen cabinets. But just as I was going into the kitchen to make myself a snack, I heard a loud stage whisper from the broom closet by the door.

"*Psst!* In here."

I looked around, to make sure I wasn't imagining things. But the voice really was coming from the broom closet. I opened the door and there was Sara-Beth, all curled up, reading with a flashlight in the dark. She was wearing this off-the-shoulder Versace top with a pair of my old pajama pants, and she was sitting on top of one of her special woven-hemp meditation pillows. She had a pile of papers on her lap.

"How was your first day?" she whispered.

"Sara-Beth," I whispered back, "what are you doing in there?"

"Studying."

"In the broom closet?"

"I don't want to get distracted."

"Are you going to sleep over again tonight?" I asked, going over to the fridge for a Nantucket Nectar. Sara-Beth had apparently ordered FreshDirect while I was in class, because there was a bunch of weird stuff in there: bok choy and kale and what looked like the biggest turnip I'd ever seen. I wondered why she'd bothered. I seriously doubted that she knew how to cook.

"Yes. No. I don't know." She covered her face with her hands. "Oh, Flan, it's so exhausting. I tried to check into the Sherry-Netherland this afternoon, but a paparazzo vaulted past these security guards and chased me into the lobby."

"Really? That's terrible."

"Well, it goes with the territory, I guess." She made a face. "And at least I fought him off! I think the only picture he managed to take was of me swinging my purse toward his camera. His lens was pretty much out of commission after that."

I laughed sympathetically. "So what are you studying now? Self-defense?"

"No, for my meeting with the board. My broker gave me this list of questions they might ask." She sighed. "But like I said, it's too exhausting. I just can't concentrate."

"Well, I have to study too," I offered. "Maybe we could study together."

"Could we?" Sara-Beth grinned. "You always have the best ideas."

I convinced Sara-Beth that we'd really be more comfortable in the living room—even as small as she is, the closet is a tight squeeze—so a few minutes later we were sitting on the couch with our notebooks and pens all over the coffee table. I started working on my algebra stuff, but even though I'm usually really good at math, I couldn't focus. Maybe it was because every few minutes, Sara-Beth squeezed her eyes shut and started mumbling to herself, like she was trying to recite something she'd memorized.

"Do you want me to quiz you?" I finally asked.

"Oh, I don't know. I'm not sure I know my lines yet."

"Don't worry about it. You'll do fine." I took the broker's cheat sheet out of her hand. "So, pretend I'm the board, and you're you."

"Wait, wait. I need to center myself first." Sara-Beth took a deep breath and looked down. Then she looked up again, with this kind of strange, blank expression on her face. "All right, go."

"Okay." I looked down at the sheet. Sara-Beth had doodled all kinds of things in the margins, like her initials in 3-D and big dark eyes crying. I read the first question. "What impact do you think your celebrity status would have on the other residents of the building?"

"I'm not so much of a celebrity, really," she said, her voice all soft and sincere. "Just think of me as a normal teenage girl . . . who's divorced her parents and needs a humble little three-bedroom to call her own."

"Hang on a minute. You divorced your parents?"

"Oh, years ago." Her eyes narrowed. "Those snakes. They were after my fortune. And after that one party with Leland Brinker and the cast of *Survivor* ended up in all the papers, they wouldn't let me have my friends over to the house."

I looked back down at the cheat sheet. "Do *not* mention the *Survivor* party," it said in red marker next to the first question.

"Maybe you should say something else instead," I suggested. "Like, 'Oh, sure I'm a celebrity, but I'm not going to, you know, throw huge crazy parties that end up in the *National Enquirer*. That's not my thing anymore.'"

"Oh yeah! That's so much better, Flan." Sara-Beth's eyes got wide. "Why didn't I think of that?"

I shrugged. "Okay, next question. How do you plan to deter the paparazzi from staking out your residence?"

"Ha! I'd like to see them try. Two words: pepper spray."

"Mace is considered a concealed weapon in New York State," I read from the cheat sheet.

"Shoot!" Sara-Beth snapped her fingers.

"Yeah, that's tough." I looked on down the list to the next question. "What do you think you could offer the community at 820 Fifth Avenue?"

"That's easy. Celebrity spotting. How else are they going to see Nick Lachey in their elevator at four in the morning?" She smiled dreamily. "Of course, my *heart* belongs to David. . . ."

I didn't even have to look at the cheat sheet this time.

"Listen, if you keep telling them how famous you are, there's no way they're going to approve you. I mean, it's stupid or whatever, but that's just how it is."

Sara-Beth's lower lip got all trembly and she looked like she was about to cry. "So you're saying that if I try to get to know them—if I tell them stories from my life—you don't think they'll like me?"

"Of course they will. Everyone likes you, Sara-Beth," I added quickly.

She sniffled. "I have a big fan base in Korea, you know."

"I just mean you don't have to keep reminding them you're a celebrity."

"But I don't want to lie."

"Well, but this isn't really like lying." I thought of my lunch with Judith and Meredith and all the things I hadn't said. "I mean, you're just, you know, not showing them every side there is to you. That's not the same as making stuff up. When you live in the building, they'll probably find out everything else anyway."

"I guess that's true." Sara-Beth nodded solemnly. "I'll have to be like Cinderella. Disguised as ordinary, but still a princess inside."

"Cinderella was an orphan. I don't think she was really a princess."

"Of course she was. How else did she have a fairy godmother?"

"I'm pretty sure the fairy godmother just felt sorry for her. Wasn't Cinderella, like, a chimney sweep or something?"

"That's gross."

"Well, after she married the prince, she probably

became a princess." I handed her the cheat sheet back. She studied it sadly.

"Poor Cinderella. I hope he didn't make her sign a prenup." She folded it in half. "Thanks so much for all your help, Flan."

I shrugged. "Don't mention it."

"But I mean it, I really do. Before, I was so worried, but now I feel . . . at peace. I'm sure I'll get the apartment now." She smiled tranquilly. "Maybe you're like my fairy godmother."

"Bippity boppity boo," I joked, and tapped her cute nose with the eraser on my pencil.

Just then, her cell phone started ringing upstairs. Even though the TV show ended about four years ago, SBB's ringtone is still the theme song from *Mike's Princesses*.

"Shouldn't you get that?" I asked after it rang about five times.

"Oh, I'll let it go to voice mail." One second later, the doorbell rang and Sara-Beth dove behind the couch. "They're here!" she squealed, terrified.

I went to the door and looked through the peephole. Sara-Beth must have been rubbing off on me, because I was almost expecting a team of paparazzi or that creepy guy who'd stalked Jodie Foster to be standing on our stoop. Instead, though, it was a very cheerful-looking woman in a pink Chanel suit, holding a clipboard. A white stretch limo was parked in front of a fire hydrant outside our building. I opened the door really slowly. Too late, I realized I should have kept the chain on.

"Can I help you?"

"I'm here to collect Sara-Beth."

"Excuse me?" I crossed my arms and tried to look tough. "She's not here. You have the wrong—"

Before I could even get the words out, though, Sara-Beth was squeezing past me out the door. In the time it had taken me to answer the door, she had changed into a shiny black dress with a big bow on one shoulder, and heels. She looked totally glammed out.

"I'm so sorry, Flan, I forgot." Sara-Beth glanced back over her shoulder as she scurried toward the limo. "Kisses!"

I blinked. "Wait, where are you going?"

"Photo shoot! Don't wait up for me! And remember, if anyone asks, I'm not even here!"

As the limo sped away, I felt really weird and kind of sad. My movie star friend was sprinting off to some crazy glamorous night out, and the two nicest girls I'd met at school were probably hanging out together in one of their homes, eating Tostitos and being all happy and normal. Which left me on my own, doing homework. I wasn't famous, but I wasn't normal either. I was stuck in between. As great as it was having Sara-Beth over, it wasn't much fun keeping her secrets. I already had enough of my own.

Chapter 7

The first week of school was over, so Meredith, Judith, and I decided to celebrate by going to a coffee shop called the Bean Garden right around the corner from my house. I love that place. It has free wireless and these cute little outdoor café tables that look like something you might see in France, plus every kind of flavored coffee imaginable—hazelnut, banana, even pumpkin pie. That Friday, I was already sipping my cup of white chocolate mocha when Meredith and Judith finally settled on their flavors. Carrying our coffee cups, we walked to the tables outside.

"This place is so cute, Flan," said Meredith, biting into the lemon-poppy-seed muffin she'd just bought. "Thanks so much for bringing us."

"Yeah, I love it here," I said. "My sister used to come here all the time when she was in high school to do homework and stuff, and after a while I just started coming along with her."

"I didn't know you had a sister," said Judith. "What's she do?"

"I'm not exactly sure," I admitted. "I think she's helping this friend of hers make a music video in Brooklyn, so she's been staying out there for a few days."

"Wow, that's so cool." Meredith smiled and I could see the little poppy seeds stuck between her teeth.

"How'd she get your parents' permission to go do that?" asked Judith, sipping her gingerbread-flavored latte. "My mom would freak out if she thought I was partying with musicians all night."

"Well, they're not partying. They're filming," I said. The minute I said it, I wondered why I was trying to protect Feb from accusations of partying. She'd be the last person to come to her own defense. "Besides, my folks are pretty laid-back. They'd probably think of it as an educational experience." *If they know*, I added to myself.

I didn't mean to be dishonest with Judith and Meredith, but sometimes I found myself trying so hard to act "normal" that these weird little defensive half-truths came out before I could even think about it. I don't like to lie, so every time it happened, I found myself feeling lousy and awkward. The worst part of it was that the better I got to know them, the more I did it. Part of it was the situation with SBB—she'd ended up staying with me all week, so whenever I hung around with Judith and Meredith after school, I had to keep thinking of new excuses for why they couldn't come over to my house. But now it was starting to develop into a full-blown bad habit.

"Hey, so did I tell you guys about what happened in English class today?" Meredith asked. All week, she'd been sharing stories about her crazy English teacher, Mr. Franklin. I hadn't seen him yet, but according to Meredith he was shaped like a gumdrop and wore taps on his shoes. "We were talking about this Robert Burns poem, and all of a sudden Mr. F started *singing* it. I mean, really belting it out. Apparently it's the lyrics to a folk song or something, but he just started singing it, randomly, right in the middle of the discussion."

"Does he have a nice voice?" asked Judith.

Meredith giggled. "*He* thinks so anyway."

I smiled, and was about to join in their conversation myself, when I looked up and saw Sara-Beth Benny walking down the sidewalk toward us. She wasn't very recognizable—this time she had on a Farrah Fawcett–type seventies wig, a sweat suit, and no makeup to speak of—but I knew it was her right away, maybe because she was dragging her feet in this sad way that she does whenever she gets upset. From her eyes, it looked a little bit like she'd been crying.

I wanted to stop her and ask her what was wrong, but I was afraid that if I went and talked to her, or even said hello, Judith and Meredith and everyone around would figure out who she was and make a big scene. So instead of jumping up and going to her, I did just the opposite: I tried to turn my chair so she wouldn't see me, and pretended to be really absorbed in whatever my friends were talking about. Even at the time, I felt awful about it, but when Sara-Beth passed by without seeing us, I breathed a sigh of relief, even though I still wasn't sure what I was so afraid of.

*T*his was really fun," said Meredith as we picked up our purses and threw our coffee cups in the trash.

"It's such a cute neighborhood too," said Judith. "Is your house really just right around the corner from here?"

"It's pretty close, yeah," I said, navigating my way between tables back to the sidewalk. I felt nervous and a little guilty, because I kind of knew they thought it was weird I hadn't asked them over. I didn't want to keep making excuses, but after seeing SBB headed in the direction of my house—and in tears—I didn't know what to do. I tried to change the subject by saying, "So what are you guys doing this weekend?" but Judith ignored it.

"Oh, nothing much. Anyway, since we're right here, we might as well walk you home. I'd love to see Flan's mysterious house—wouldn't you, Meredith?"

"It's not mysterious," I said. "It's just kind of a mess. Between the renovations and the leak . . ."

"Sure. I bet it's like one of those old haunted mansions from *Scooby-Doo*." Meredith giggled. "Stop worrying! I'm sure it's beautiful, Flan."

"Don't be so embarrassed," said Judith. "It's this way, right?" She strode forward purposefully, slipping out to cross the street between two parked cars.

So as we walked toward my house, even though I was trying to laugh and make conversation like usual, I had the uncomfortable feeling that criminals must have when they're being trailed by the police—the feeling that I was about to get busted. As we walked past apartment buildings, an antique store, a little juice bar, even a dingy subway stop, I found myself wishing I were going anywhere but home.

The three of us turned onto Perry Street and walked under trees with leaves just starting to change. Meredith and Judith cooed over the funky touches my neighbors had added to their town houses: a stained-glass window that showed two blue figures dancing around the sun, a window box that overflowed with creeping vines, a balcony decorated with white icicle Christmas lights.

"That's the Eastons'," I said. "They're old and sort

of crazy, I think. They used to have a light-up Santa up there too, before the bad windstorm."

"Do you know all your neighbors?" asked Meredith. "We've been living in my building for three years and I hardly know any of mine."

"It's a pretty friendly neighborhood, I guess," I said, even though that wasn't strictly true. Actually, I'd met most of the neighbors when they'd come to complain about the noise coming from Patch's parties in the early hours of the morning. Over the years, I'd gotten very familiar with seeing my neighbors angry and in their pajamas. "This one's mine."

We walked up the steps to my front door. I bought a little time by fumbling with my keys while I tried to figure out what to do. I didn't want to lie to Meredith and Judith—or worse yet, make them feel like I didn't want to have them over—but what was I supposed to do? SBB was going nuts in there, and if I brought in a couple of people she'd never met, she'd probably go completely psycho on them. And finding America's favorite starlet a teary, howling mess in my living room would probably make them wonder what else I was hiding, not to mention make them never want to hang out with me again. So I did the only thing I could: I panicked.

"Listen," I said, half-turning with my key in the

lock. "I'm really, really sorry, but I just can't have you guys over right now. I promised I wouldn't have anyone over and . . . my family'll get really mad if I do."

Meredith and Judith looked up at me, totally speechless and confused. I opened the door. I wanted to tell them more—reassure them that I still liked them and stuff—but I felt like I'd already said too much. So instead I just added, "Things are just complicated right now. But I'll see you on Monday, okay? I promise."

Before they could say anything, I went inside and shut the door behind me. For a minute, I just stood there, feeling as crappy as I ever have in my life. Things had been going so well with my new friends, and I'd totally blown them off. My face was burning hot and I felt sick. I promised myself that I'd text them later in the evening—maybe I could explain the situation better if I had a little time to think about it first.

But there was no time to replay it in my head just then, because I had been right: Sara-Beth Benny *was* a teary mess. She was lying on the sofa right in the middle of the living room, covered with balled-up Kleenexes, and she had so much running mascara around her eyes that she looked like a wild raccoon. She'd changed from her sweat suit into a pair of True

Religion jeans and a T-shirt that had a silk-screened cartoon kitten on it, crying its eyes out into its furry paws. That was the good thing about having eight closets' worth of clothes—she really did have an outfit for every occasion.

"Sara-Beth," I said, "what happened? Are you okay?"

Sara-Beth looked over at me and sniffled. "Oh, Flan, I'm so glad you're finally here," she said. "The worst thing in the world just happened. The co-op board rejected me."

"What? Why?" I went over and sat down in a chair across from her. "Maybe you misunderstood something. That doesn't make any sense. They haven't even interviewed you yet. I didn't even get a chance to write you a recommendation."

"I know. They flat-out rejected my application. They called me today and said they thought me living there would make the place too . . . 'chaotic.' That was the word they used." SBB sat up, and dozens of wadded-up tissues avalanched to the floor. "I think it was the cover of *Us Weekly* that did it. The photographer got that shot right outside of my last apartment."

I felt really, really sad for Sara-Beth. After all, this was beyond unfair—she'd never wanted those pictures to get taken. Even if she had divorced her parents and thrown a party so over the top that it had wound up on an episode of *E!: America's Wildest Parties,* she still deserved a nice place to live—or at least a fair chance at getting one. For a second, I imagined how weird it would be if I didn't have the house on Perry Street to come home to, with all its familiar furniture and nice memories. But I couldn't even wrap my mind around how lonely that would make me.

"You know, Sara-Beth," I heard myself say, "you can stay here for a while, if you want. Until you find another place."

"Oh, could I? I promise I won't be any trouble at all. Thank you. Thank you so much! I can hardly wait." Sara-Beth leapt off the sofa. "I'll be back in one hour with my trunks!"

"Trunks?"

"If that's all right. I like the old steamer trunks, you know? They're so charming and old-fashioned."

I nodded. "Okay, sure."

"But there's just one more eensy little thing I need to ask. If I'm going to stay . . ." Sara-Beth paused. "You can't tell anyone, even your friends, that I'm here. If the news gets out that I'm here, the paparazzi will swarm—absolutely swarm—and then I'll never get into a co-op."

"All right," I said. But there was a sinking feeling in my stomach that told me it would be anything but.

Chapter 9

*E*ven though I'd promised myself that I would text-message Meredith and Judith to somehow give them a better idea of what was going on, I couldn't bring myself to do it. What would I say if I couldn't explain about Sara-Beth Benny and her weird housing situation? I'd just have to make up more lies, and I didn't want to do that. So instead, I spent the weekend doodling sad faces in the margins of my history textbook, wondering if Meredith and Judith would completely shun me on Monday morning. They didn't call or text me, which I took as a pretty bad sign. Fortunately, I had SBB to keep me company, so I wasn't totally miserable. On Sunday afternoon, we made pink lemonade and watched *Some Like It Hot*, which did a lot to help cheer me up.

On Monday, I was pretty nervous when I went looking for Meredith and Judith down by the subway stop. I kept checking my watch, all paranoid that they'd decided to take a different route to avoid me or something. But when they finally came up the stairs, they didn't look angry to see me there—more just wary than anything else, I thought.

"Hey," I said, awkwardly tugging on my backpack straps. "I was starting to think I'd missed you guys."

Judith sighed. "No, it's more like we almost missed you. Gorgeous here forgot to put her contacts in this morning, and we were almost ready to get on the train when she realized we had to go back."

Meredith rolled her eyes at Judith affectionately, like she was used to getting razzed. "But who takes about two hours to blow her hair dry, huh?"

"You guys walk to the subway together every day?" I asked as we started walking to school.

"Practically every morning," said Judith. "We barely live a block away from each other. Guess that's why we were so curious about your house—we don't know anyone who lives downtown."

I took a deep breath. "I wanted to apologize to you guys about that—"

"No, no." Meredith smiled with her little teeth and tossed a quarter into a street musician's saxophone case. "Don't worry about it. Like I said to Judith on the way home, we were the ones being nosy."

"No, you weren't. Not at all. My place is just a disaster right now."

I was glad we'd at least talked about it a little, but I hated keeping secrets. The whole rest of the way to school, I kept feeling like they were sneaking suspicious glances in my direction.

Fortunately, Meredith and Judith weren't too mad to eat lunch with me, so we all walked together from fourth period to go stand in the lunch line together. That day, the food in the cafeteria was particularly gross. They had a bunch of cold things every day—yogurt, apples, bagels—but only one hot lunch, and that day it was Tater Tot casserole. I'd never seen anything quite like it. It was gray and soupy, with soggy little clots of potato scattered around in it like they were plastic packing peanuts thrown in there by mistake. Most of the people ahead of me in line were letting the old lady with plastic bags on her hands glop it onto their plates, which I couldn't quite believe. Once I saw that Meredith and Judith had decided on salads and bagels instead, I joked, "Check it out. The Iron Chef's here, and the secret ingredient is crap."

Meredith laughed—and so did the guy behind me in the lunch line. I turned around and almost jumped out of my skin. He was wearing jeans, a red polo shirt, and these really cute John Fluevog shoes that looked like they were stolen from a bowling alley, and his eyes were crinkled up with laughter. And it was him: Bennett Keating, the second-cutest boy in tenth grade.

"I know," he said. "I forgot my lunch too. It's so stupid—surrounded by all these good restaurants, and we're stuck eating this."

"Y-yeah," I stammered, willing myself not to blush. "It's really ridiculous."

"I'm Bennett." He offered me his hand to shake but, like an idiot, I was still holding my tray. "I don't think I've seen you around before."

"Oh. Well, I just started here. I mean, I'm a freshman. My name's Flan."

"How're you liking this place so far, Flan?"

"It's nice." I wished I could stop sounding so boring. I grabbed a bagel and set it on my tray, then held a paper cup under the soda machine and pressed a button. A fine spray of Dr. Pepper got all over me, but fortunately Bennett didn't seem to notice. "I mean, the people here seem really cool. It's great how many student clubs and activities there are and stuff."

"I think so. Some people find it really hard to navigate at first, though." He cleared his throat. "I'm actually doing a piece for the school paper about the new class's impressions of Stuyvesant."

"Really?"

"Yeah. Maybe I could interview you?"

"Sure!" I tried not to squeak.

"What're you doing after school?"

"Um . . ." I glanced toward Meredith and Judith, who had fallen totally silent—out of shyness or because Bennett was flirting with me, I couldn't tell which. "The three of us usually hang out, so—"

"Well, then, we should all go get some ice cream. We deserve it after this lunch. There's a great place right around here—Cones, have you ever heard of it?"

"Wow, I love that place." Cones was an adorable little ice cream shop just a couple of blocks from my house. "Meredith, Judith—you want to go after school?"

They nodded silently, each wearing a big smile.

"All right. Nice to meet you guys," he said, sailing off into the cafeteria with his tray. As soon as he was out of earshot, Meredith and Judith practically exploded with whispers.

"That was so awesome!" Meredith cheered into my ear. "Oh my God, Flan, he really likes you! That was like love at first sight!"

"And he has tons of cute friends! This is so amazing!" Judith was so happy, she was nearly jumping up and down.

My luck couldn't have been better. Two totally

wonderful things had just happened at once. First, Bennett had asked me out, and second, Meredith and Judith had started trusting me again. This was turning into an amazing day—and all because of Tater Tot casserole. Who'd have thought?

On the way out of the cafeteria, Bennett stopped by our table with two of his friends: that snobby guy Eric (who mentioned twice that he was entering some male modeling competition, even though I could tell by one look at him that he needed some major manscaping—at least an eyebrow wax and a better haircut—before he could even *think* about being in print ads) and this other kid, Jules, who was kind of heavyset but had cool black-framed glasses that made him look like he was in an emo band.

When school was over, we all met at the front entrance and walked out together. It was great, leaving school with three cute guys, and I started to feel like maybe I wasn't such a loser after all.

In fact, I was more worried about Meredith and Judith. As soon as the guys showed up to meet us, they started to get all giggly and only talk to each other. I've seen girls act like that before, but I've never quite gotten it: you can know a girl who's totally cool, funny, whatever, but as soon as you put her into the same room as a cute guy, she suddenly will only giggle and whisper to her best friend like she's nine years old, and no one watching her would ever be able to guess that she's actually an interesting person. Then again, I've known lots of seemingly normal guys who burp and tell dirty jokes to impress the girls they like, so I guess it goes both ways.

"So, do you guys all work on the *Spectator*?" I asked.

Eric rolled his eyes. "Journalism, ugh. What's the point? Since when do people want to see pictures of drowned cows and starving babies?"

"That's not really what we focus on in the school paper," Bennett said.

"I'm the photographer," said Jules, "and I made a rule for myself to keep drowned cows and starving babies to a minimum."

"Unless it's a story about the cafeteria food," Bennett joked, glancing at me with a flirty smile. I laughed. Meredith and Judith were way ahead of us on the sidewalk by now.

At Cones, we got a table near the window. I ordered mint chocolate chip, and Bennett paid for it. I wondered if that made it a date, but before I could overanalyze it too much, Jules started telling this crazy story about his West Highland terrier and how she managed to get inside his building's ventilation system.

"The people downstairs thought a giant rat was coming after them. And we were like, 'No, that's just Muffy.'"

"I wish I had a dog," I said. "The last time I had a pet was when I was in fifth grade. She was a chinchilla."

"What happened to her?" asked Bennett.

"Don't ask," I sighed. Zsa-Zsa had actually crawled down the stairs during one of my brother's parties, only to be crushed under the wheels of a Vespa that Patch's friend Mickey had driven into our house. Mickey had felt terrible about it, and he'd made up to me by hiring a skywriter he knew to write, "SORRY PATCH'S LI'L SIS" in the sky.

"You didn't finish your story, Jules," said Meredith shyly, stealing a glance over at him. I could tell she liked him because of how she kept pushing her cup of ice cream around the table with her spoon. "I hope your dog was okay."

"She was fine. But we had to pay to get the claw marks hammered out of the air ducts."

We sat there for maybe half an hour, talking and laughing and joking around. I noticed after a while that Bennett's elbow was touching mine on the table. But I didn't move my arm, and neither did he. It was awesome.

When we were all packing up our stuff to leave, Bennett sort of lingered, putting on his hooded sweatshirt and zipping it up slowly, like he was waiting for something.

"Hey, Flan," he said, "remember how I'm writing that article for the *Spectator*? About freshmen at our school?"

Between the ice cream and the flirting and the joking around, I'd actually forgotten. But instead I said, "Yeah, sure," as I slung my backpack up onto my shoulders.

"Well, I didn't really interview you yet. Where do you live? I could ask you some questions on the way to your house."

"Oh," I said. A sick feeling crept into my stomach and curled up there. "Well, I mean—I guess—"

Meredith and Judith looked at me with these "oh

my God, what are you doing" sort of expressions on their faces.

"Hang on just a sec," said Judith, grabbing me by my elbow. "I want to show you something." She dragged me over to the glass case that held all the flavors of ice cream. Meredith followed us. "What are you doing?" Judith hissed at me as we stared down at a carton of butter pecan. "I mean, you're shy, okay, I get that, but think about it! This is huge—Bennett Keating wants to walk you home!"

"That sure looks delicious," I said loudly, for the benefit of the guys who were awkwardly standing around the little shop's entrance. Then I whispered, "I don't know. I just feel like it's maybe . . . too soon. I barely know him."

"Too soon to walk around with him? That's how you get to know someone!" It was pretty ironic that she was getting so worked up about this, considering the fact that she and Meredith had been practically mute the whole time we'd been hanging out with the guys. I almost said so, then stopped myself at the last second.

"He seems pretty nice," Meredith added in an undertone. "I don't think he's going to start stalking you or anything. But I know how you feel. I've never hung out with a guy by myself either."

I shook my head, thinking of Jonathan, my ex, and all the time we'd spent talking up in my room while parties raged below. "No, that's not really the prob—"

"Then just do it!" Judith gave me a little push and I stumbled back in Bennett's direction, just as someone appeared behind the counter to offer me a free sample of butter pecan.

"Okay," I said, smiling at Bennett as best I was able. "Let's get going." But as we walked out to the street, I flipped open my cell phone and texted SBB as quickly as I could. ON MY WAY HOME, I wrote. STAY OUTTA SIGHT.

So Bennett walked me home. His survey only took about ten minutes, because he forgot some of the questions and he also forgot to write down any of my answers, which I thought was totally cute. Either he was really absentminded, or being around me made him shy, which seemed more likely, the way he kept looking over at me and then looking away again when I made eye contact. I'd never been with a guy who was actually shyer than I was, and it kind of surprised me how much I liked getting him to talk. It's sort of like how SBB calms me down by being more freaked out than I am—quiet people bring me more out of myself. I even cracked a few jokes and got to hear him laugh, which was great. His laugh was even cuter than his voice.

The one weird thing about the walk was the way he kept trying to impress me.

"I really like the Village," he said. We were taking a kind of long way back to my house, which was just fine by me. "It's a fun place to hang out. You see that club over there?"

"Oh yeah." I nodded. He was pointing at Turquoise, this dance club that was really hot a little over a year ago before it got kind of lame and touristy. I'd been there a lot in junior high when my brother was on the VIP list. My favorite part was an area toward the back, behind the artificial waterfall, where you could sit and watch people dancing through the constantly spilling water. I'd mostly hung out there, drinking Shirley Temples and talking with Jonathan about stupid stuff while everyone else bumped and ground around like crazy animals. At the end of one evening, this one girl had gotten up on the bar and started stripping and dancing around, but they were afraid to pull her down because she was wearing these really insanely tall stiletto heels, so most of the guys just hooted and took pictures of her with their cell phones. And then eventually they formed a net with their hands and she jumped and they all caught her.

"Yeah, my sister's boyfriend's best friend works behind the bar," he said shyly. "One time I went there and hung out with them. It's a cool scene. It was kind of empty that night—quiet, you know, but really chill. Maybe I could get us in there again, if you wanted to see it. But we'd probably have to sneak in through the back."

"Cool," I said, looking down at my shoes. I felt kind of bad, like I should tell him I'd already been there a million times, but I felt like that might make him embarrassed.

We walked on toward my house, and I started thinking that Bennett had planned to take me the long way on purpose, because he kept telling me stories about every little place we passed.

"Hey, check it out," he said when we walked past a comic book shop. "I saw Zen Wemble here one time— do you know who that guy is? He created this character named Boulderman for Marvel. I heard they're making it into a movie with Josh Hartnett. Anyway, Wemble was doing a signing and I even got to talk to him for a couple minutes. He was really down-to-earth, really friendly."

"That's so cool," I said. "Do you like comic books a lot?"

"Sure. *X-Men*, *Batman*, all that stuff." Bennett

gazed longingly into the window of the shop as we passed. A bunch of little action figures were set up on display in a scale model of Gotham. "But, you know, I read regular books too. It's not like I'm one of those creepy comic book guys who has a life-size model of the Blonde Phantom."

"You mean you don't have a safe full of vintage comics still in their original sleeves?" I joked. "Or Spider-Man pajamas?"

Bennett didn't meet my eyes. "No, of course not."

And it was weird, because with every story he told me about how interesting his life was, the more normal and kind of sweet he seemed. I couldn't remember the last time I'd heard a guy brag about seeing a celebrity or not getting carded, because all the guys I knew either *were* celebrities or hung around with them enough to be on the VIP list. But most of those guys were annoying flirts who had better relationships with the salespeople at Barneys than with their girlfriends. And then I looked up and found we were already in front of my house.

"Well, I guess I better get going," I said, starting up the steps.

"Sure," said Bennett. "I guess I'll see you."

"Okay." I took out my keys and started to unlock the door. But then Bennett came a little closer, so he was standing right behind me. I turned back around and felt myself starting to blush. My heart felt like it might explode. Was he going to kiss me?

I looked into Bennett's eyes. They were gray and really pretty, sort of like stones that have gotten worn down by the waves on a beach. He had a bunch of freckles on his nose.

"I guess I'll see you at school tomorrow," he said.

"Okay." We stood there for a long moment, not even an arm's length away from each other. Bennett ran his hand through his hair a few times. Finally, I felt really awkward and turned to go in the door. But right then he moved forward. His mouth bumped into my ear, and I hit him in the chest with my shoulder.

"Ow!"

"Sorry, sorry," he mumbled.

"No, no, it's really okay. I'm sorry."

"Sorry."

"No, I—"

"Yeah, okay, see you." And he took off down the block, leaving me standing on my front steps, shaking my head. I was so unprepared for all this.

Chapter 11

Oh my God!" Sara-Beth squealed, leaping up from where she was crouched at the living room window. "That was the cutest first kiss I've ever seen. It was so real and awkward and . . . real!"

"It wasn't *my* first kiss. Jonathan kissed me when we were going out—and hey, why were you watching me?" I set down my stuff on the floor. It was sort of creepy that she was peeping out of the curtains like that.

"I look out the window all day. I don't want to get taken by surprise. Besides, you told me to hide out. I wanted to know what I was hiding from." She folded her arms across her chest. "Now, don't change the subject, Flan. Who is this boy? Why haven't you told me about him?"

"You keep being at photo shoots in the evenings. Anyway, I only really started hanging out with him today." I looked away. The truth was, I hadn't talked to SBB much about high school at all. With her glamorous life, I figured she couldn't offer me much good advice anyway. How could she not be clueless about normal teenagers, when she'd basically lived in a bubble?

"Well, that kiss was the greatest thing I've ever seen. It was so genuine. I wish my first kiss had been like that."

"It wasn't my first kiss."

"Whatever. It looked totally unrehearsed, and that's what counts." Sara-Beth sighed. "My first kiss was in front of a live studio audience." She flipped open her cell phone and started scrolling through her address book. "Listen, we need to go out and celebrate. How do you like Italian food?"

"Sara-Beth, I have school tomorrow."

"Good point. All that starch would make your face puffy. How do you feel about Swedish? I'll treat."

"Okay, okay." I walked into the kitchen to pour myself a glass of water. "Hey, there's a message on the machine. You know who it's from?"

"Oh, Philippa Frady. I think it's for Patch. She sounded kind of upset." I was about to play the message, but then SBB poked a new button on her phone and started making dinner reservations.

So we ended up going to this crazy little restaurant where they served different-colored globs of herring on stone plates and everyone was very somber like they are in old black-and-white Swedish films. After a really intense conversation about Sara-Beth's phobias and her search for a new shrink—she'd decided she couldn't keep going to David's parents, since she planned to marry their son—"And there are certain things you don't want the grandparents of your kids to know!"— we both needed some cheering up.

So Sara-Beth took me to this hot new club in the East Village, Cube, where the floor lights up in all these crazy multicolored squares. It kind of reminded me of Dance Dance Revolution or maybe Twister, the way people were bending over backwards and twining around one another, but way cooler. Sara-Beth yelled something at me I couldn't hear as we went in, so I went and squeezed in at the very end of the bar where it was quieter while she got us drinks and came over to sit with me. She'd gotten a Cosmopolitan for herself, but for me she'd picked something that looked like a green milk shake in a martini glass.

"It's a Grasshopper," she said. We could actually hear each other now, which was definitely an improvement. I took a little sip. It tasted like a Thin Mint in liquid form, but I knew I shouldn't drink the rest of it. My brother and sister let me drink beers every once in a while, but I never have on a school night. Still, it was pretty cool to be sitting there with Sara-Beth in this way-trendy club, with our girly cocktails and the floor lighting up.

"This is so much fun," I told her, tucking my hair behind my ears. Just as I said it, my cell phone rang. I flipped it open. It was Judith. "I'll be right back," I told SBB.

Somehow, amid all the flashing lights, I found my way to the women's bathroom. It was fairly quiet in there. As I dialed Judith's number, I hoped she wouldn't be able to hear the club noises in the background.

"Hey," I said, trying to sound as school-night normal as I possibly could. "What's up, Judith?"

"Flan! I'm so glad you answered. I didn't wake you up, did I?"

I looked at my watch—it was almost midnight. "No. I was . . . in the shower."

"Cool. So what happened with Bennett? I'm dying to hear all the details!"

"Oh." I rubbed my ear thoughtfully. Somehow it seemed mean to tell her what had happened. I thought of her and Meredith giggling and hesitated. I didn't want Bennett to be embarrassed. "He's really sweet."

"Yeah? Do you think he likes you?"

"Maybe. I hope so. I definitely like him."

"What did you guys talk about?"

"The usual stuff. He collects comic books." I faked a yawn. "Hey, listen, I really better crash. I'm glad you called, though."

"Okay. But you better give me the juicy stuff tomorrow!"

I hurried back out into the club, worried I'd find SBB lonely and forlorn, hunched over her drink. But when I got back, she wasn't alone at all. This other girl—very tall, very blond, very East Side—was sitting right next to her at the bar. I recognized her immediately, of course. Her name was Liesel Reid, and all of Manhattan had been at her sweet sixteen party earlier in the summer. In fact, that was where I'd met SBB. Liesel had ridden into the ballroom on a white horse in this Michael Kors eyelet dress, and she'd looked exactly like a princess. Which, of course, she was.

Liesel hadn't changed at all since the last time I'd seen her, except tonight she had her gold hair piled up on top of her head and she was wearing a Diane von Furstenberg dress with matching gloves. On anyone else, it might have looked old-fashioned, but on her it was just sophisticated and right.

"Hey," I said, slipping back up onto my bar stool. "Remember me?"

Liesel gasped. "Flan! My darling little Flan Flood! You're so grown up, I hardly recognized you!" The truth was, Liesel had seen me just three months earlier, at my fourteenth birthday party, which she'd helped to plan. I didn't think I'd changed much since then, but hey, you never know. She offered a gloved hand for me to shake. "How *is* Patch?"

"He's fine," I said, feeling like the lame little sister again all of a sudden. It made sense that she'd ask, though. She used to go out with another one of Patch's friends, Arno, who was almost as beautiful and fashion-conscious as she was, and she knew Patch pretty well too.

Liesel ordered a brandy Alexander. The bartender disappeared.

"I hope to God he gets it right this time," Liesel said, rolling her eyes. "Last night he got the proportions all wrong. Bartending is an art form. Mixology, it's called. I wish people would take it seriously."

"You've been coming here a lot?" I asked tentatively.

"Darling, I have to. It's my job." The bartender came back and gave her the drink. He looked kind of nervous until she took a sip, shook her head, and handed the glass back to him. "I'm a promoter. I keep the club chic, classy, and exclusive."

"How do you do that?" I asked.

"By just being here, of course." Liesel scanned the room. "They offered to pay me, you know, but I consider it philanthropy. This place was an absolute *hole* before I started coming in. Now, Sara-Beth, I thought you were in Gdansk."

"I don't even want to talk about it," SBB said. "Ric Roderickson is a lunatic. He wouldn't even keep my masseuse on call."

"I know, snookums, he's a tyrant." Liesel kept scanning the room. I guessed she was looking for unchic people. I held my Grasshopper close and tried to look as cool as possible.

"Look at that," Liesel hissed suddenly. She cut her eyes across the room, and we turned to see.

About a dozen feet away, a model in baggy ripped jeans, flip-flops, and a weathered Mickey Mouse baby tee was shouldering up to the bar. She had short, spiky blond hair, and she was yelling, "Who do you have to sleep with to get a drink in this hellhole?" while she rooted around in her fanny pack for cash. She used her elbows to get through the crowd, knocking drinks over and making green apple martini spill all down the front of one girl's white dress.

Under one arm, the model carried an orange Pomeranian with a red bandanna tied around his neck. The dog was squirming, trying to get away from the model and gnaw off the way-tacky neckwear, but every time he thrashed she just squeezed him harder—at one point, he even yelped. I felt sorry for the little guy. It was kind of hard to believe that such a nasty, tasteless woman would have such a cute pet.

"That bitch is trying way, way too hard," said SBB. "And I don't mean the dog."

"It's always the models," Liesel said. "They keep confusing crazy and ugly with cool." Liesel set down her drink. "Excuse me, darlings. I can't just sit here while this club's reputation gets into the E-Z Pass lane and takes the Holland Tunnel out of town. I've got a job to do."

Liesel walked toward the woman and the noise in the bar seemed to suddenly die down. Even the music got quieter. People parted to let Liesel through, and I felt like I could even hear the heels of her shoes hitting the light-up floor. When she reached the woman with the dog, she tapped her on the shoulder with one gloved finger. The model turned around, still snarling from her fight with the bartender.

"Excuse me," Liesel said. "I don't like you." She looked down at the Pomeranian, who wiggled around wildly, trying to escape. "But what's even worse is that your dog *hates* you."

Everybody started applauding. And then Liesel

took the dog right out of the model's arms and started walking back to where we were sitting. Meanwhile, two bouncers dragged the woman out, still yelling and cursing.

"That was awesome," I said as Liesel took her seat.

"All in a day's work, darling." The little dog was looking at me with his big brown eyes and waving his paws wildly in my direction, like he wanted me to pick him up. "Now you, he likes."

"He's adorable."

"He's yours." Liesel handed him to me, and the dog started licking my face. He made little high-pitched noises in his throat and snuffled at my hair.

"Oh, I couldn't take him," I said. "It wouldn't be right."

"I think he'll be much happier with you than with that other lady," said Sara-Beth. The little dog squealed like he was agreeing.

"Consider him a gift," said Liesel.

I would have said no, and maybe I should have, but the little guy was staring at me with his huge eyes all wide and kind of crazy with love. Besides, I didn't want to make Liesel mad. She could probably have turned my social life to ice with just one look. And I thought I remembered my mom saying that if someone gives you a present, you better take it.

So I untied the dog's ugly bandanna and took him home. On the way back, Sara-Beth and I stopped for bubble teas at this Asian place right by my house, and the waitress liked the little dog so much that she gave him a plate of lo mein. When I was watching him wolf it down, I decided to name him Noodles.

By the time we finally got to Perry Street, it was too late to even think straight, but I felt happy just the same. Now all I wanted to do was fall down on my bed and go to sleep. But when we walked through the door, we banged right up against three enormous suitcases, and they definitely did not belong to my parents.

Chapter 12

*P*hilippa Frady," I gasped. "What are you doing here?"

"I called earlier. Didn't you get my message?" Philippa was sitting on the couch, with mascara-stained Kleenexes piled up all around her. She was wearing a pair of tight, charcoal-colored Diesel jeans and a wifebeater tank top, and her usually light brown hair was dyed a kind of maroon color and cut so the ends looked all jagged and wild. She looked like a badass with a broken heart.

I've known Philippa Frady for a while, from a distance, because she went to grade school with SBB and because, for as long as anyone can remember, practically, she's had this on-again, off-again relationship with Mickey Pardo, one of my brother's best friends and her next-door neighbor. I've always kind of admired Philippa because she's like a younger, taller version of Jennifer Connelly, with long brown hair and this kind of downtown, artsy vibe to her. She's really chill and ironic and laid-back—laid-back about everything except for her relationship, that is.

See, ages ago, I guess that Mickey's father, who is a sculptor, got in a big fight with Philippa's father, an art dealer, over this big piece that he was supposed to buy from him or something. Nobody really knows the details, and probably the two sets of parents don't even remember anymore, but the end result is that they hate each other and never ever want their kids to be dating. So Mickey and Philippa are like Romeo and Juliet, because they always have to keep it a secret when they're going out. For a while it seemed like they were actually broken up for good, because Philippa announced that she was a lesbian, but then she broke up with this way-irritating girl she was seeing and decided she wanted to be with Mickey again after all.

It was a weird situation, but I really admired how Philippa went out and reinvented herself and tried something crazy and different and risky. I don't think I'm going to start dating girls anytime soon, but I know in my life how important it is to change and experiment with stuff, so I guess I always kind of looked up to Philippa for giving the lesbian thing a try.

Anyway, none of this explained why she was sitting

in my living room, crying, in the middle of the night. I was so surprised to see her there that I dropped Noodles, who quickly scrambled across the living room. He jumped onto her lap and tried to lick away her tears.

"Down, down, little guy!" Philippa pushed at Noodles, laughing a little despite herself. "Why does your dog smell like Chinese food?"

Before I could answer, Patch came out of the kitchen, eating a sandwich.

"Hey, sis," he said as he went up the stairs. "New dog?"

"Yeah. So what's going on here?"

"Philippa ran away from home," Patch yelled down the stairs. "I guess she'll crash with us for a while."

I nodded, still confused. "What happened?"

"I had a terrible fight with my folks," Philippa said, staring down into her lap. "God, it was so unbeliev-able. We were all just beginning to speak to one another again, and then when they found Mickey sleeping in my bedroom, they just totally—"

"Flipped out? Oh, I could tell you some stories." Sara-Beth flung herself down on the couch dramati-cally. "It's a horrible thing, having a mom and a dad."

"Yeah. They can be such assholes." Philippa blew her nose loudly. SBB nodded.

"And those snakes are out for every cent they can get," SBB said. "That's why you're going to need a good lawyer—the best."

I thought of Judith's father. Maybe I could send some business his way.

"But I'm not just mad at them. I'm pissed at Mickey too. He totally bailed on me. He thinks this is all just a big joke." Philippa slumped back on the couch. "The minute they found him, he was out the window. Literally. He sprained his ankle! Sometimes I think he doesn't care about me at all—he just likes me because I'm a challenge. First he can't have me because of my folks, then he can't have me because I'm into girls. But whoo-flippin'-hoo, once he gets me, he just totally flakes out. He just treats me like a girlfriend, not like a real friend, you know?"

"That's terrible." I sat down on the couch. It sort of sounded like Philippa was overreacting—Mickey was a good guy, from what I knew about him—but then again I hadn't heard the whole story. Noodles jumped into my lap and I scratched his belly. "So let me get this straight: your parents found Mickey in your room, Mickey totally bailed on you, and you came here to get away from all of them?"

"Basically, yeah. Plus my parents might be suing the Pardos, but that's a whole other issue. Sorry to burden you guys." Philippa covered her face with her hands. "It's all a huge mess. I just need someone to talk to, I guess."

"I love these late-night chats." Sara-Beth grinned. "It's like a sleepover."

"It kind of is." But I could barely keep my eyes open. Even Noodles was falling asleep in my lap. I dragged myself up off the sofa before I could pass out, and held my sleeping dog like a baby. "Hey, I've got school tomorrow, but you two should keep hanging out."

"Do you want to?" Philippa looked at SBB all sorrowfully. "I should warn you that I'm not going to be much fun. I'll probably just keep talking about my problems all night."

"Of course I'll stay up with you! But on one condition." Sara-Beth looked up at me. "Flan, can we have a blanket fort?"

"Sure, I won't stop you. There's a closet full of blankets and throws right off the pantry." I carried Noodles upstairs, put on my pajamas, and crawled into bed. I was exhausted. Down below I could hear Philippa crying while Sara-Beth knocked over furniture and rummaged through the linen closet, but even if she was breaking everything in the house, I was way too tired to care.

* * *

In the morning, I woke up with Noodles licking my face. He really was the cutest thing I'd ever seen. Pomeranians have these funny little mouths that make them look like they're smiling all the time. I spent a long time just petting him before I made myself get out of bed and start getting ready for school. The minute I started trying to move, I understood why most of us don't party like rock stars during the week. It's one thing to stay up if you don't have anything to do the next day, but if you have first-period algebra to look forward to, it's another situation entirely.

I could tell SBB and Philippa had stayed up even later than I did, because even though I was banging around the kitchen, trying to figure out how to make the coffee I normally don't drink, they didn't make a sound. Sara-Beth really had rigged up a blanket fort, using the leather wingback chairs from my dad's study and what looked like the entire contents of the linen closet. It looked like an elephant was sleeping under a patchwork quilt, right in the middle of our living room.

I finally choked down some granola and the coffee-flavored water I'd managed to make, and I boiled some spaghetti for Noodles, who was standing on his hind legs and waving his paws around excitedly. I promised him that I'd buy him some dog food after school, then stumbled out the door. As I walked, I realized there was no way I'd be able to keep this up for long. Normal by day, fabulous by night only really ever works for superheroes—for the rest of us, it always falls apart sooner or later.

On my way to second period, I went up three escalators, pushed through a crowd of thousands, and found Meredith and Judith waiting outside my classroom. Fortunately, they were way too giggly and excited to notice how wiped out I was.

"Oh my God, did you hear?" Meredith asked me. "A bunch of the sophomores are having a big party this weekend. It's going to be excellent."

"Okay . . ." I looked from Judith's face to Meredith's and back. "But we're not sophomores."

"We might as well be!" Judith squealed. "Check it out!"

She thrust a folded-up piece of notebook paper at me. My name was written on it in Sharpie, with a single zigzag line drawn under it, like the person who wrote it was trying to make his handwriting look macho and sharp. I unfolded the note.

The message was written in pen:

> *Hey, Flan, I just happened to be passing by your locker and thought I'd let you know there's a party you, M., and J. might be interested in this weekend. It's going to be mostly sophomores, so you might not know everyone there, but it should be chill anyway. It's on Friday night at my friend Devon's place in Chelsea. Call me for details. Here's my cell.*

He'd put down his cell phone number, his landline, his e-mail, and his AIM. Then he'd signed off— *Bennett*—with the zigzag underline. There was a PS too:

> *It was cool talking to you yesterday. Give me a call.*

Even though the party sounded cool and everything, I was also kind of cracking up inside. It was so cute and funny how Bennett had put down every possible way of contacting him and asking me to call. Twice. But even if it was kind of silly, it also melted my heart. When I looked back up at Meredith and Judith, though, they were just grinning at me like I was holding a winning lottery ticket.

"Did you read it?" asked Judith. "Isn't that amaz-ing?"

"Wait a second, how did you get this note?" I asked. I was not getting a lot of privacy lately: first Sara-Beth was spying on me out of the window—now my school friends were reading my mail.

"We passed by your locker," Meredith explained. "Bennett was about to stick it through the vents in your door, but he figured you'd be more likely to get it if we brought it to you. He did mention the party to us too."

"Okay." I folded it up and put it back in my pocket. For a moment I was suspicious that they'd opened the note but then I figured it was easier to just believe them. At least he hadn't mentioned anything about the ear-kiss. I wanted to keep that to myself.

It was weird: I'd always been a really open, honest person, but since starting high school I suddenly had a lot of secrets. I had to hide Sara-Beth, because I'd promised to, and now that Philippa had run away to our house, I probably wasn't supposed to tell anyone that she was there either. But I was also keeping a bunch of stuff about myself secret: the fact that my parents didn't work, all the parties and craziness that went on at my house, my celebrity friends, my nights out on the town. I even felt weird mentioning my old boyfriend, Jonathan, to Judith and Meredith, since they seemed to have had practically no experience with guys. And now I was hiding the ear-kiss too—supposedly to protect Bennett, but really more to protect myself. Enough was enough. I opened my mouth to tell Judith and Meredith about it, about anything and everything, but at just that second, Bennett walked by.

"Hey," he said. "You got my note?"

"Yep." I held it up, and he flashed me a dazzling smile.

"I've gotta run to class. But I'll talk to you later, right?"

"I'll call you."

Bennett disappeared down the hallway, and before he was even out of earshot, Meredith and Judith hugged each other.

"This is going to be the coolest weekend ever," Judith said. "Hey, listen, we should all go over to your place to get ready before the party, Flan. We can do one another's hair."

I hesitated, but fortunately, before I had to think of another excuse, Meredith jumped in.

"No, we should meet at my place, and I'll help dress you guys up," Meredith said. "No offense, Flan, but I think I have more accessories than both of you and Bloomingdale's put together."

I had to stop myself from breathing a sigh of relief. "That's cool."

We decided that after the party we should sleep over at Judith's because, as she pointed out, her bedroom had two big beds and a comfy couch, and she had her own TV. With cable. I wasn't about to argue.

The rest of the day, I sleepwalked around Stuyvesant. It's really a huge school, not even in the same league as Miss Mallard's. And even though the hallways are all sterile and white and kind of same-looking, it's important to learn the geography, just so you don't wind up stumbling into the middle of the wrong clique and making a fool of yourself. On the second floor, for example, there's the Cuddle Puddle, a group of senior guys and girls who lounge around on the floor or each other's laps, and the first time I was up there I practically tripped over them. Then, up on the third floor, a bunch of Asian juniors hang out in the atrium. Some sketchy, punked-out kids lurk around the fourth-floor escalator, and on the fifth floor a lot of drama geeks are always singing and dancing and practicing their lines for performing-arts class.

Walking around the school that day was like being in a dream, and I found myself wondering where I fit in. It was weird: even though I'd been trying to reinvent myself, I hadn't really found out what I wanted or liked yet. I'd been too busy hiding old stuff about myself to uncover anything new. I didn't want to end up just traveling around and goofing off forever, like my parents, but I still didn't know what I *did* want to be. I decided that from now on, I'd try harder to figure it out. After all, I was growing up—it was time to get serious.

The *Spectator* had a meeting after school that day, so I wasn't surprised that Bennett didn't offer to walk me home. In fact, it was even kind of nice to walk back to the house by myself. This way I didn't have anything to worry about, anyone to impress—or anyone trying to impress me. I could just go along at my own pace, thinking about stuff and being myself. I picked up a bag of dog food and some squeak toys at a pet-care shop near our house and walked along with the shopping bag on my arm, feeling very grown-up and relaxed—almost as mellow as Patch can be sometimes. In fact, I was pretty happy right up until the minute that I opened the door and discovered that we had yet another uninvited houseguest living under our roof.

"Liesel Reid!" I gasped. "What are you doing here?"

Liesel was standing in the middle of the living room, surrounded by designer dresses on silver racks like you might see in a department store. Noodles was running around her feet, yapping and standing on his hind legs like he was in the circus or something. I guess he recognized her from the night before.

"Flan, darling!" Liesel air-kissed me from across the room. "Sara-Beth told me about the delightful time you've all been having. I just *had* to see the scene with my own eyes."

"I figured she could sleep upstairs with you, since I'm staying in the blanket fort from now on," said Sara-Beth, walking down the stairs in the multicolored Stella McCartney minidress I'd worn to my eighth-grade graduation. It was all baggy on her, and the hem hung down way past her knees.

"Then where's Philippa going to sleep?" I asked, pushing Noodles down off my legs. I guess the little guy smelled dog food in the bag I was carrying, because he was going sort of crazy.

"I thought I'd stay in the attic," said Philippa, walking into the living room holding a six-pack of Patch's PBR. She was wearing the same pair of charcoal jeans from yesterday, and her maroon hair was twisted up tight into a tiny, messy bun. Her mascara looked blurry. She popped open one of the beers.

"It's kind of early for that, don't you think?" I asked, scooping up Noodles into my arms.

"Yeah, you know, I'm trying to build up a tolerance." Philippa swigged from the can and involuntarily made a face. "The guys—Mickey anyway—can drink five of these in a row. It's lame that I get tipsy after just one. If I want Mickey to really respect me like a friend, I need to get tougher. More independent, you know? Start doing things on my own."

"Like drinking?" I didn't know quite what else to say. It was cool that she was so into being her own person, but somehow I didn't like the idea of her drinking a bunch of beers by herself. It seemed kind of sad. And gross. That stuff tastes like ginger ale with a dash of gasoline. Plus, if she wanted to be so independent, why was she just copying what Mickey's friends did?

Philippa set the beer can on the coffee table. "Not just drinking. Did I tell you I'm getting a motorcycle?"

"Really?"

"Yup. I'm getting off the back of Mickey's Vespa once and for all."

"Snookums, do you have an extra closet I could use?" Liesel was organizing her dresses by color. "Because I'm afraid these shoulders might stretch."

"There might be one upstairs. I can try to find—"

Sara-Beth spun around and clapped her hands, like she always does when she's in a room full of people who aren't paying attention to her. "But Flan, first you have to coach me. My real estate agent says I might have a chance at another building, and you're the only one who really understands—"

"Wait, wasn't I talking?" Philippa folded her arms; if I didn't know better, I would have thought she looked a little jealous. "You've monopolized Flan for the last week and a half, Sara-Beth. Give someone else a turn. I hadn't even told her about the Harley yet."

"Okay, everybody just hang on a second." I went into the kitchen, tore open the bag of dog food, and poured it into a cereal bowl for Noodles. Then I pressed my hands to my temples, counted to five, and went back out to the living room. The second I stepped out there, all three of them started talking at once again, but I waved my arms around all crazily, like I was landing a plane, until I got them to stop.

"Listen, I want to listen to everybody, but I still don't know what Liesel's doing here. So I need to hear that first."

"Oh, Flan, I thought you'd never ask. You'll appreciate this."

"It *is* quite a story," said Philippa, making herself swallow a mouthful of beer.

"Did you see my air horn? It's for self-defense." Sara-Beth grabbed a weird, tiny megaphone from behind the couch, and it released a blast of deafening sound.

Once we could all hear again, Liesel went on with her story.

"You see, my parents have hired this very chic, very avant-garde painter, Jean Bologne—do you know his work?—to paint a mural all throughout our penthouse, except on the windows, of course, because that would spoil our views of the park. I was all for this little arts-and-crafts project when it began, but once Jean started his painting, he began making certain—advances. Small things at first: a new vial of L'Eau d'Oiseau would pop up on my vanity, a Limoges box heart would appear in my purse, a bottle of champagne would arrive while I was throwing a party with friends." She shivered. "But as if that wasn't creepy enough, things took a turn for the stalkerish when he actually started to paint the mural in my bedroom. It looked like a simple woodland scene at first, but then a nymph started to emerge from the brush. A wood nymph, naked as the day she was born. A nymph who looked"—and here a look of creeped-out horror crossed her face, and she lowered her voice to a whisper—"a lot like me."

"Artists," said Philippa cynically, leaning back and putting her feet up on the coffee table. She looked ready to fall asleep, and she hadn't even finished her first Pabst. "Believe me, I've seen a lot of them. My family collects art, you know. And Mickey's dad sculpts—"

"I know, darling," said Liesel, patting Philippa's shoulder affectionately, like they'd both survived the same terrible disease or something. "I know." She turned back to me. "So you see, I couldn't stay there. And when I told Sara-Beth about it, she said she knew you'd want me to stay here instead. Of course I just couldn't believe it at first, but she went on and on about how absolutely generous you are, and how you'd never leave me out in the cold, so thank you Flan, thank you so much!"

"Well . . . I'm glad you found your way here okay," I stammered.

Sara-Beth was inviting people to stay with us now?

"Now will you quiz me for the board meeting, Flan?" asked SBB. She waved a handful of flash cards at me. "I've been making these all day."

"Look, I promise I'll help you. Just give me a couple of hours to start on my own homework, okay?" I felt really tired all of a sudden.

"What?" she asked.

"Just a little while?"

"Did you say *hours*?" Sara-Beth screeched. She stormed off in the direction of the broom closet. I thought about following her, then reconsidered and slung my backpack up onto my shoulders. As I went up the stairs, though, Liesel called up after me.

"Flan! Flan! There's just one more little thing."

"What's that?"

"Do me an enormous favor, and don't tell anyone I'm here. If my parents find out, they'll send the car around for me in an instant." Liesel ran her hand down a rack of dresses contentedly. "But if no one tells them, they won't even notice I'm gone."

"All right."

"Don't tell anybody about me either," Philippa added as I climbed the stairs. "I don't want my parents—or Mickey—to find me." She paused. "Not both at the same time anyway."

Up in my bedroom, I glanced around. SBB had set up all these Styrofoam heads with her wigs on them; their blank faces stared down at me from the shelves and I felt surrounded. I dropped my heavy backpack onto my bed. Noodles, who had followed me up the stairs, pranced around my ankles, and I sat down to let him lick my face. I didn't know exactly why I felt so stressed out, but I sure did. I kept trying to remind myself that I had three of the coolest girls in Manhattan living right there in my house, but it still felt funny.

It was weird having to keep them all a secret, but it was more than that. They all seemed so . . . so needy. Which was totally bizarre, from my perspective. Who'd have thought I'd have Liesel Reid, Philippa Frady, *and* Sara-Beth Benny asking me for advice, when I still was having awkward ear-kisses and mooning over sophomore boys? These girls were cool, beautiful, and stylish, with awesome Insider boys going crazy over them, and I was basically a wallflower in heels—even if my last name *was* Flood. To me, it was like some Alice in Wonderland thing where everything's backward. I promised myself, then and there, that I'd have my own life figured out better by the time I was seventeen. What was the point of being awesome and older if you still couldn't manage your own life?

I set Noodles down on the ground, unzipped my backpack, and sat down at my desk to start in on my American history homework. But just as I got absorbed in a new section on the Iroquois tribes, I heard the unmistakable blast of Sara-Beth's air horn, followed by a crash.

I ran down the stairs, half-expecting to see Sara-Beth in the grasp of a paparazzo. But instead I found the three girls standing around the shattered pieces of a glass vase. I couldn't believe it. My parents had gotten it in Finland from some crazy glass artist who had stuff in the Met. Despite all the parties my brother had thrown, he'd never once broken something so expensive. Then again, there was the time when Mickey rode his Vespa into the house and burned up the carpet—and that weird incident when Arno got his tongue frozen to a really expensive one-of-a-kind ice sculpture that Mr. Pardo had made for my parents and we had to call the paramedics to get him loose. But still, this was not what I wanted to find when I got to the bottom of the stairs.

"What happened?" I asked. My voice came out more like a squeak, but the girls heard it well enough.

"Sara-Beth—closet—air horn—I just jumped up," Philippa sputtered. "I thought there was a fire or something."

"Liesel tried to scare me! She was making camera sounds right outside the closet door."

"I was not! You should know by now, my Hermès bag clicks when it opens." Liesel whirled around on Philippa. "If you weren't ripped, I mean terribly, you would have looked where you were going!"

"Oh yeah?" Philippa lunged at Liesel. Sara-Beth pulled them apart. Her skinny arms were surprisingly strong.

"Wait, wait, wait." I shook my head in disbelief. These girls were older than me? They were acting like kindergartners. "You guys, this is crazy. I'm not mad at anyone, okay? Obviously, it was an accident."

All three girls looked at me suspiciously.

"You mean it?" said Philippa. "You're not mad?"

"No. I mean, it's going to be hard explaining this to my parents. . . ." I looked down at the shards. "But I know it wasn't anyone's fault."

"So we can stay?" asked Liesel breathlessly.

"If you all apologize," I offered. "Not to me, to one another."

The three girls stared at their feet.

"Sorry," they murmured in unison.

Liesel and I cleaned up the broken glass while Philippa poured out the rest of her can of Pabst and Sara-Beth exiled herself to the closet. When I went upstairs, it was really quiet, almost like little kids were having a time-out. On one hand, I wanted to congratulate myself for keeping everyone from killing one another, but on the other I felt really worried. What was my house turning into? Flan Flood's Home for Wayward Girls?

Chapter 15

Over the next few days, things continued to fall apart around my house. I'm not just talking about lamps shattering, slammed doors coming off their hinges, or doggy tooth marks showing up on the leather upholstery, although all that happened too. I'm talking about SBB, Philippa, and Liesel systematically going out of their minds.

Sometimes the girls fought like crazy, and sometimes they got along like best friends. By Friday, I wasn't sure which was worse. It was awful to try to do homework with them screaming and yelling at one another, but it was also horrible to listen to them booing the contestants on *America's Next Top Model*, cackling like crazy bag ladies, and popping open the corks of champagne bottles from my parents' wine collection.

The house was getting messier every day. Sara-Beth's

rice crisps were all crunched down between the cushions of the red leather sofa, Philippa's mascara was smeared on every pillowcase in the house, and Liesel's neatly folded blouses kept appearing on every available shelf, including the ones in the refrigerator, since she couldn't find enough closet space to hold them all.

By Wednesday, the only time I was able to chill out was at school, and even then I kept getting distracted during class, wondering what new disaster I'd walk into the minute I stepped through my front door. None of them appeared to be going to classes at all, and I sometimes wondered if I'd see a team of truant officers leading them away in handcuffs. Then again, I kept forgetting that they were all a lot older than me. Maybe by the time you're a senior, and famous, nobody makes you go to school.

I still had to get up every morning and drag myself to first-period algebra, though, and in spite of everything, that less insane portion of my life seemed to be going pretty well. Judith and Meredith were really excited about the party on Friday, and I was starting to get psyched for it too. First we were going to meet up at Meredith's around seven, then head over to the party around nine. (The party actually started at 8:30, but Judith kept repeating the words "fashionably late" like she'd discovered plutonium or something. I didn't mind, though—I don't think I've showed up for a party on time once in my life.) After that, we were going to go to Judith's, stay up late, and watch movies. I couldn't wait. Not only was I going to hang out with my new, normal friends, I might even have a chance at a decent night's sleep. That wasn't really possible at my house, with Noodles barking and Sara-Beth flipping the lights on and off all night as she tried on my clothes.

By the time Friday afternoon rolled around, I just wanted to throw some stuff in an overnight bag and get out of the house as quickly as possible. I didn't particularly want to tell Liesel, Philippa, or SBB about the party, but it ended up slipping out anyway, when Sara-Beth walked in on me putting my toothbrush in its plastic case.

"What do you *mean* you're going to a party?" she demanded, reaching past me for her jar of nutmeg body butter.

"With people from school. Listen, don't be so mad. I didn't think you'd be interested, that's all." I took my retainer out of the medicine cabinet—I'm still supposed to wear it at night. "I mean, it's not a big deal. I'm just going to this one guy's apartment and then afterwards I'm sleeping over with some friends."

SBB's eyes got wide and scared. "You mean, you're not coming home *at all* tonight?"

"Well, I'll be back early tomorr—"

"Liesel! Philippa!" Sara-Beth screamed.

Once I got Sara-Beth to stop sobbing, though, it turned out that all three of the girls were really interested in the party. Liesel couldn't believe it was going to be at someone's apartment—"Couldn't they book a larger venue?" Philippa wanted to come along, incognito, to test out a new party scene sans Mickey.

"It's mostly going to be sophomores," I explained. She raked her fingers through her hair, which she'd dyed black to match her new motorcycle jacket.

"I wouldn't mind being the older woman for a change," she said.

SBB wanted to know if it would be like *Rock U,* the short-lived spin-off series one of her "sisters" from *Mike's Princesses* had gone on to create. "Is this a kegger?" she demanded. "I think they were sophomores in that show."

"Sophomores in *college*," I explained. "These are people from my high school."

After I'd survived the interrogation—and convinced all three of them that they'd probably have a better time staying home than tagging along with me—they decided that the least they could do was help me dress up. I'm not sure they were so bent on making me look nice, either. Now that the initial excitement of hearing about my plans was over, all three of them seemed pretty focused on telling me their problems and getting my advice. For Liesel, her old, superstylish boyfriend Arno was back on the scene, and she was trying to decide if they could spend a weekend in Acapulco together without him flirting with thong-wearing skanks the whole time. Philippa had finally broken down and called Mickey, and from the way she was talking about him, it seemed like she was thinking of asking him to move into the attic with her, even though that was my sister February's room and Feb was supposed to be back any time now (I still hadn't heard how that music video of hers turned out). And Sara-Beth was flipping out completely, because her real estate agent still hadn't found another building for her to try. It was all pretty intense.

"So I said, 'Arno, darling, let's go back to the Riviera.' And he of course said, 'But it's like the Riviera—of Mexico.' I mean, tell me honestly, Flan. You're a good judge of character. Can I rely on this boy for anything at all?"

"This is unbelievable—I've been waiting by the phone all afternoon. Am I going to have to live out of a suitcase for the rest of my life? Don't these people know who I am?"

"Of course he'd already bought the tickets, but that's no excuse. There's no excuse for refusing to change your plans."

"It'd be cool to set up house with Mickey—you know, not in the June Cleaver pre-feminist way, but like, just to spend time with him. Get away from all the drama with our parents, you know? Do you think it'd be okay if he stayed over a couple of days, just to test it out?"

"If I didn't have you, Flan, I'd be lost—cast out onto the street. The little match girl. Did you know I played her once, in a Discover commercial?"

It went on like that for about an hour. In between their long complaints about everything, the girls fought over how to dress me up. Philippa wanted me to wear a pair of my sister's old knee-high Doc Martens and a kickboxing T-shirt embellished with rhinestones that I'd picked up from a shop in Soho mostly as a joke. Sara-Beth wanted to glam me up in this powder-blue tank dress—she even offered to loan me some of the borrowed jewelry she'd worn to the Oscars and then never returned—and Liesel thought I should go for a classy look in this white Monique Lhuillier dress of hers that made me look like I was trying to be a taller, chestier version of Audrey Hepburn.

All of this seemed like a terrible idea to me, and in the end I wound up throwing on this halter-neck dress I'd been wearing all summer. It was pink with little white hearts printed all over it in patterns, and it was made of a T-shirty material, so I looked nice but not psychotically overdressed.

When I came out of the bedroom with it on, though, all three of my houseguests looked at me like I'd just killed somebody.

"You're totally caving to this outdated notion of femininity," said Philippa.

"Your shoes don't match your purse," said Liesel.

"Oh, Flan," said Sara-Beth. "You look so . . . unassuming."

"Okay," I said. "I guess I better get going."

The girls still stood there, though, right in the middle of the hallway. Like a wall.

"'Scuse me," I said, shouldering past them.

"Have a nice time," Philippa called after me as I started down the stairs.

"Thanks." She sounded so sad that I couldn't help feeling bad about leaving them like this. I turned around. "I'm sorry I didn't tell you about the party sooner. Maybe next time I can get you all invited too."

"Come on, Flan, we know you're totally ashamed of us." Philippa smiled darkly. "Seriously, don't worry about it. Have a good time."

I shifted my overnight bag onto my shoulder. "What are you guys going to do while I'm gone?"

"Oh, you know. Old boring spinsters, home alone on a Friday night," Liesel said, gesturing vaguely. "We'll find some way to entertain ourselves."

"Uh-huh," I said as I let myself out of the house and locked the door behind me. But as I walked to the corner to hail a cab, I couldn't help but wonder what exactly would go down while I was away. I knew Philippa, SBB, and Liesel well enough by now to know that they weren't going to spend the evening playing Monopoly and eating popcorn. I just hoped the house would still be in one piece by the time I got back.

Chapter 16

By the time I made it over to Meredith's house, I was starting to feel excited about the party again. There's something so great and exciting about taking a cab by yourself and watching all the streets go by, knowing you can get out anytime or keep going for as long as you want, knowing that no one's going to stop you or tell you what to do. I felt bad at first about leaving Liesel, Philippa, and SBB alone while I went out on the town, but as I rode along, it occurred to me that I really shouldn't feel too guilty. After all, what Philippa had said touched on the truth: if they came out with me, it would totally blow their cover. Besides, it wasn't like SBB invited me along on her photo shoots. Everyone keeps parts of their lives separate sometimes. It didn't make me a phony or a bad friend—at least, that was what I wanted to believe.

Anyway, the point is, when I got out of the cab and

lugged my suitcase up to Meredith's door, my heart was feeling lighter and I was even starting to smile a little bit. Maybe this night wouldn't be such a disaster after all. The doorman let me in and even tipped his cap as I walked by. I love it when they do that.

Meredith lived in an older building, with a small, clanking elevator that seemed to take forever to get from the ground to the second floor, where her apartment was. When the elevator doors opened, I took a deep breath and stepped into the hallway. Here it was: the start of my first big night out as a normal high schooler. Tucking my hair behind my ears, I walked down the hall to apartment 2B and knocked.

Meredith and Judith were both already there, and they came to the door together.

"Oh my God, you look so pretty," said Meredith, stepping aside so I could come in. "Let me take your bag."

"Oh, no, that's okay," I said awkwardly as she took it out of my hands and went down the hallway. Judith rolled her eyes.

"Meredith's the perfect hostess," she said. "Trust me, there's no stopping her."

Even if Judith was being sarcastic, it really was almost true. Meredith's apartment was sort of tiny, but in an adorable, cozy kind of way, and you could tell she'd set up for us coming over. In the living room, which had orange walls so it felt sunshiny even though it was dark outside, she had a bunch of snacks—homemade cookies and kettle-cooked chips and hummus and pita bread—all laid out on the coffee table, and in the corner of the room an ice cream maker was buzzing as it churned. I suddenly realized I was starving—I hadn't eaten anything since the yogurt I'd had for lunch in the cafeteria that day.

"Meredith, this is so nice," I called down the hall to her. "You didn't have to go to so much trouble."

"Oh, it's no trouble. We worked on it together," said a kindly old lady, coming out of what I guessed was the kitchen with a dish towel. She had short gray hair and glasses, and she was wearing this really cool turquoise dress with oversize yellow buttons that I could tell she'd made herself. "I'm Meredith's grandma. You can call me Amelia."

"It's nice to meet you," I said, shaking her hand. The way her eyes crinkled up when she smiled reminded me of Mrs. Santa Claus.

"Meredith's mother is doing inventory over at the shop, but I suppose you'll meet her later when you come by to pick up your bags."

"I live just down the block," Judith explained, making herself comfortable on the couch, which was this vintage-looking red velvet thing, "so I figured you and Meredith could just leave your sleeping bags and stuff here till after the party. Then we can come back here and pick them up."

"It's so great that you live right by each other," I said, feeling jealous. How cool would it be to hang out here all the time? The whole place smelled like cookies.

I sat on the couch with Judith. After a few minutes Meredith came out and we all sat around, scarfing down hummus and talking about our classes together at school. It was so great to just be hanging out with people who weren't all having nervous breakdowns and totally depending on me to set things right. Meredith did a great imitation of her English teacher, and Judith and I both cracked up. Then I told them about my history teacher, who was sort of obsessed with the Kennedy assassination, and they thought it was pretty funny too. Then the conversation turned to boys.

"That was almost as funny as Meredith's story," Judith said when she stopped laughing. She ate a chip. "You should tell that one to Bennett."

"Well, he's a sophomore. He probably knows Mr. Martin already."

"God, Flan, Bennett's so cute." Meredith went over to the ice cream maker and started spooning out mugfuls for each of us. I saw it was mint chocolate chip—my favorite. "It's awesome he likes you so much."

"Yeah, well, maybe he doesn't like me *that* much."

"No way! You know, I bet at the party tonight he won't talk to any other girls," said Meredith.

"What would you do if he asked you to be his girl-friend?" asked Judith.

I felt embarrassed for some reason, and I took a long minute to swallow my first bite of ice cream. "I doubt that'll happen. I mean, he practically just met me."

"I think it just seems like it won't happen because it hasn't yet." Meredith plopped back down on the couch. "But I bet we'll all have boyfriends someday."

"I went out with a guy once," said Judith. "Well, I mean, not literally went out. He's the son of these friends of my parents and he goes to boarding school in New Hampshire. But we were pen pals for a while. So, I mean, it's not totally hopeless."

"I remember that guy." Meredith grinned. "He sent you that bracelet in the mail, with the little charm of a pelican on it."

I thought about Jonathan, my ex, and decided to spill the beans. That was one secret I didn't have to keep anyway. "I kind of went out with this guy once, back in eighth grade."

"Really?" asked Judith and Meredith at the same time.

This was it: I had to tell them all about him—how we met, how we used to hang out in my room during Patch's crazy parties, how he used to take me out to clubs and compliment my shoes. Otherwise, I would be being dishonest for real, and for no other reason than being afraid of what they might think. But with them both looking at me so eagerly like that, I just couldn't do it. So I looked down at my spoon instead.

"He was okay, but we never got to spend that much time together. He was more into hanging out with his friends."

"What was it like, though?" Judith pressed, leaning her elbows on the coffee table. "Did you guys hold hands and stuff? Or did you mostly just talk on the phone?"

"Did you ever dance with him?" asked Meredith, crunching on a carrot stick.

I tried to think of a good story. "Well, this one time, at Lotus—"

"Wait, Lotus?" Judith sat back and scrutinized me. "You mean, that club in the Village? The one that's, like, impossible to get into?"

I shrugged. "It's not impossible. He was . . ." I wanted to explain about the Insiders, the way they have a free pass to pretty much anyplace in the city, but it all just seemed too complicated all of a sudden, and I knew in my heart Meredith and Judith just wouldn't understand. "You know, he was older."

They both stared at me, sort of awed and freaked out at the same time, like I'd just confessed to being Catwoman or something.

"Wow," said Meredith.

After an awkward silence, we decided that even if we were going to be fashionably late, we might as well go ahead and get ready. So we all went back to Meredith's room to put on accessories and do one another's hair.

Meredith's room was really tiny—a closet, practically—but it was super colorful, with bright green chiffon-y curtains hanging down around the bed and a bunch of paintings she'd done all over the walls. In a corner of the room she had a little yellow desk, and along with all the books and papers she had for class there was half a rainbow-colored sweater that she was crocheting.

She had tons of accessories too: big beaded necklaces and little jingly charm bracelets, batiked silk scarves and skinny leather belts. I settled on wearing just one necklace she'd made out of a lot of little vintage buttons, but Judith ended up putting on a bunch of scarves and bracelets that made her simple tank-top-and-jeans outfit look way more exotic, almost like a belly dancer's or something. Then Judith did Meredith's makeup in such a way that it brought out her eyes and cheekbones, without looking fake or overdone at all. It was amazing the way Meredith and Judith complemented each other; it made me a little jealous, even. I've had a lot of best friends, but never one who brought out all my best qualities like that. Maybe if I got to know the two of them better, I thought, they'd have the same effect on me.

Meredith changed her outfit like five times until she settled on this neat patchwork sundress that she and her mom had made together sometime during the summer. Then we were all ready to go. We said good-bye to Meredith's grandma, went outside and down to the corner, and I stepped off the curb to hail another cab.

We really could just take the subway, you know," said Judith as a yellow taxi came to a stop in front of us. "That would probably be cheaper."

"No, there're three of us. So it's the same, practically," said Meredith, opening the door. "Flan's right—this makes more sense."

I climbed in after Meredith. Judith got in and told the driver the address, and pretty soon we were speeding toward the party. I looked at my watch: 8:15. So much for fashionably late. We'd be lucky if we weren't early.

"I hope Jules is there," Meredith sighed, looking out the window of the cab. "He's cute."

"Not as cute as Eric," Judith pointed out.

"I thought you said he was a snob," I said.

"Yeah, but when he's as cute as that, who cares? It's not like I'm going to pay attention to anything he says anyway."

"Well, Jules likes animals. Remember that story he told about his dog? I think that's a cute quality in a guy."

"Listen, there're going to be a million guys at this party way cuter than Jules. I'm sure at least one of them will have a gerbil or something." Judith flipped her hair back.

I laughed, and Meredith rolled her eyes and looked back out the window.

Even though Bennett had invited us to the party, he wasn't the one throwing it. It was actually being thrown by this other sophomore guy, Devon, who lived in a high-rise in Chelsea. Chelsea is a weird part of town, especially at night, and especially around the Flower District. Sixth Avenue is okay, but all the little side streets are lined with these weird wholesale shops filled with novelty sunglasses and belt buckles and crazy little battery-operated toys that light up and play off-key music when you push a button. After about six P.M., these places all shut down and you might as well be walking through a ghost town made of iron gates and padlocks. Plus, most of the restaurants close early because they mainly just do a lunch business for all the office workers in the area. Sometimes you'll find an ice cream shop or a pizza place to go to, but not often.

So, when we got out of the cab in front of that guy Devon's building, it was spooky and deserted, and Meredith, Judith, and I decided the hell with being fashionably late, and walked into his building.

It was really pretty inside and much friendlier looking than the empty street. The lobby was huge, with a fake waterfall against one wall and lots of mirrors on the others. There was one doorman at the door and right in the middle of the lobby was a big desk with another doorman sitting at it. We told him who we were and he sent us to the elevator.

We rode up, giggling about nothing and feeling kind of nervous. I did anyway. Even though I'd been to a million high school parties with my brother and his friends, this was still my first high school party that was completely my own, and I didn't want to screw it up. Plus, going to a party with Meredith and Judith was really different than being with SBB, or Liesel, or even Jonathan. None of us was going to know very many people, and, against all odds, it seemed like I was the least shy one of the three of us.

When the elevator doors opened, though, I knew one thing for sure: at least we weren't too early. All the way down the hall I could hear people talking and laughing and the newest AFI album playing on the stereo. I walked up and, taking a deep breath, knocked on the door.

"It's open!" several voices yelled from inside.

We went in. In spite of all the noise we'd heard from down the hall, things were pretty laid-back inside. A bunch of kids were sprawled around on couches or pillows on the floor, drinking punch and talking to one another. Jules was leaning against a counter, talking intently to a long-haired guy in a pair of Birkenstocks and cargo shorts, so he didn't seem to notice us. There were a plastic tray of veggies and dip, some balloons, and paper plates with pictures of cakes on them. I hadn't realized it was Devon's birthday, but fortunately nobody seemed to have brought presents anyway.

Besides, from the look of this place, he didn't need them. The big-screen TV was rigged up with every kind of video game system known to man, way more than we even have at our house, and a pile of teenager-looking DVDs lay on the floor down below it: *School of Rock, X-Men 2, The Girl Next Door*. I didn't see how anybody could watch movies in this apartment, though—windows covered two walls, and the view was amazing.

Two guys were playing Ping-Pong at a table set up in the corner. One of them was Bennett. When he saw us, he dropped his paddle on the table and started to say hi, but his opponent, this tall thin guy in an anime T-shirt, had just served, and the plastic ball hit Bennett in the ear. What was it with him and ears?

"Hey," said Bennett, trying to act like nothing had happened. "Flan. I'm glad you could make it."

"Me too," I said, feeling sort of dopey and happy at the same time.

"You want to play doubles?" asked the anime kid, glancing at me and Meredith.

"Hey, where did Judith go?" I looked around and saw her. She was standing awkwardly behind the sofa, waiting for Eric to notice her. Unfortunately, he was sandwiched between two hot-looking sophomore girls and didn't appear to be noticing much of anything else, and Judith was too shy to talk to him. She was staring at her nails like there was no tomorrow.

Before Meredith and I could get roped into a game of Ping-Pong—which I suck at anyway—this sun-bleached-looking guy who I assumed was Devon stood up and tapped a knife on the side of his glass Coke bottle to make an announcement.

"So, guys," he said, "I know this might seem kind of junior high-ish to some of you . . ."

A few people groaned, like they knew what was coming.

"But it's a birthday tradition of mine, so just chill

out and swallow your pride." Devon downed the rest of his Coke in one gulp and, shoving aside the crudités and paper plates, set the bottle down on its side in the middle of the coffee table.

"Devon, is this the only way you can get girls to make out with you?" asked one of the hot-looking girls on the couch.

"Hey, I just go with what works. Everybody, around the table. Come on, come on. Who wants to go first?"

When everyone formed a circle, Meredith and I ended up getting pushed right up by the coffee table where the bottle was. We sat down on the carpet and looked at each other. Meredith nervously whispered, "Oh my God."

"I'll do it," said the guy in cargo shorts who'd been talking to Jules earlier. "And I don't need to trick anybody into making out with me."

A bunch of girls giggled at this, but he didn't look so bad to me—kind of cute, even, in a guy-playing-acoustic-guitar-on-a-park-bench sort of way. Still, I crossed my fingers that the bottle wouldn't spin toward me. I didn't want to end up kissing some random guy I didn't even know when I hadn't kissed Bennett right yet.

Fortunately, I didn't have to. The first time the

long-haired guy spun, the bottle turned toward Devon, who loudly protested that that didn't count. The second time, it ended up pointing to a cute black-haired girl on the other side of the coffee table who looked almost as shy as me, Meredith, and Judith. Everyone cheered, though, and even though she was blushing, she looked like she was enjoying the attention.

The long-haired guy walked over and, before she could even get up, gave her a long, friendly kiss on the mouth. It was nothing like the movies, since their lips just sort of smooshed together and they both turned their heads in the same direction, so their noses bumped into each other. But it was really sweet, in a weird way. When they'd stopped, several people applauded and hooted while the long-haired guy walked back to his corner of the room.

During all the commotion, Judith made her way over and sat down to my left, sandwiching herself in between Meredith and me. I grinned at her, and she gave a sort of "isn't this exciting" shiver. The three of us giggled and nudged one another in the ribs, when something happened that I totally wasn't expecting. From the Ping-Pong table, Bennett called out, "I'll go next!"

My first thought was, *Oh no, he's going to wind up*

making out with some other girl. But then Bennett looked over his shoulder at me all significantly as he walked over to the coffee table. Suddenly, my heart was in my throat and I could feel my palms sweating. Bennett reached out and spun the Coke bottle really slowly, like he was trying to get it to turn a certain direction, and over all the catcalls and laughs I felt like I could hear the glass sides scraping every grain of wood in the tabletop. I held my breath.

The bottle stopped, pointing between me and this red-haired girl in a Lacoste polo shirt to my right.

"Her or me, Bennett?" she teased, balancing on the arm of a chair. "Your call."

"I think it was pointing more at her," he said, looking right at me. Then he walked over, took hold of my shoulders, and kissed me very deliberately. Right. On. The. Mouth.

He whispered something to me as he took a step back, but I could hardly hear him over all the noise everyone else was making—clapping and hooting and cheering. I glanced around and saw Meredith and Judith drumming on the coffee table and yelling, "Go, Flan!" I couldn't have felt happier. This time, it was a real, bona fide kiss: there were no ears involved, and it hadn't been an accident either.

Chapter 18

When spin-the-bottle was over, we ended up sitting together in the corner of the room, on some cushions people had pulled off the couch. I can't remember what we talked about; I was feeling giddy, and I think we mostly joked around. I noticed Bennett's laugh for the first time then, the cute way he almost snorted at the end of it, but maybe I just was starting to like everything about him: his dirty-blond hair, his chipped tooth, the way he touched my arm while he was talking to me.

Bennett seemed like he could be a real boyfriend, the kind of guy who comes over for study dates and carries your books in the hallway, the sort of guy who brings lilies when you're sick and remembers your one-month anniversary. I could see us building a giant snowman together and holding hands through mittens. He was kind of awkward, and even after our big kiss it seemed like he was trying to impress me—somewhere in the midst of my daze of happiness I remember him telling a random story about how he might get to interview the Green Party gubernatorial candidate for the school paper—but I didn't care. He was a normal teenage guy, awkward and unpolished, and that was what I liked about him.

My whole relationship with Jonathan seemed like cotton candy by comparison: it looked bright and sweet, but in the end it had been totally insubstantial. I thought about our breakup, about how I'd told Jonathan that I was tired of always trying to go to the coolest clubs and impress all the hippest people, and how he said that he couldn't imagine his life without all that. It had made me cry at the time, but when Bennett kissed me a second time, on the cheek, it was just like Jonathan had never even existed. The rest of the party pretty much disappeared too. So did Liesel, Philippa, SBB, and the mess they were all making of my house. For just those few moments, I was totally content.

That night, we slept over at Judith's, and we stayed up practically all night recapping all the cool stuff that had happened: the kiss, the gossip, everything. It was totally great, and it all ended with us having one of those communal three A.M. laughing fits where you practically break your ribs from cracking up.

The next morning, Judith's mom made us challah French toast with raspberry jam and fresh-squeezed orange juice, and we all hung out until about noon. Judith's mom was really nice too. She was a good cook, and chill enough to basically ignore us while we talked. She turned slowly through the arts section of the *Times* while she ate her breakfast, then asked us about school before she went out for a run. Judith mentioned that she used to be a yoga instructor, before her dad's law practice really took off, and I could totally see it. She had that kind of Zen calm. I realized I could use some of that myself. My cell vibrated a couple of times, but I knew without looking it was SBB and I forced myself not to worry. I'd be home soon enough.

When I finally breezed into my house at about one o'clock in the afternoon, all three of my houseguests were down in the living room waiting for me. I blinked. Up to that point, I'd been all happy and exhausted, but they had such dark, accusing looks on their faces, the guilt hit me in a wave.

"Where were you? I kept calling all morning!" SBB pointed at a spot on her arm. "I was so worried, I'm getting a rash!"

"Tell us all about your new friends," said Philippa, sounding a little jealous.

"Was it fabulous, darling?" Liesel yawned, pretending not to care.

At that point, basically all I wanted to do was crash on the couch and daydream about Bennett. But, even though I wanted to keep that happy feeling all to myself for a little while longer, I realized I owed it to Liesel, Philippa, and Sara-Beth to at least tell them what went down.

"It was great," I said, sinking into a chair.

I told them everything, no holds barred: about Meredith's grandma and her cookies . . . the kiss . . . cuddling with Bennett at the party . . . sleeping over at Judith's and laughing all night. At first, it seemed like there was no way my lame little adventure would mean anything to three of the coolest, most popular senior girls in town, but as I went on, even Liesel couldn't hide the fact she was intrigued. I must have talked for almost an hour before I finally felt my eyelids starting to droop.

"God, you guys," I said, stretching, "I think I really need a nap or something. I'm wiped out."

Liesel brought me a glass of orange juice and sat down on the couch.

"Snookums, you never fail to amaze me," she said. "Who knew that high school parties could be so kitschy and fun?"

"Bennett sounds adorable." Philippa twirled a newly black strand of hair around one finger. "Like he really gets you, you know?"

"I've never been to a real high school party before," Sara-Beth confessed. "It was something I tried to work through with David's parents in therapy."

"Do you think you really could get us invited to one? Next time, I mean?" asked Philippa.

I squirmed a little. I needed to stop making promises that were so hard to keep. But what could I say?

"Sure. I can try to anyway. It would depend on who's throwing it and stuff."

"Sure." Philippa nodded.

"We wouldn't want to make it awkward for you, darling," Liesel said with a sigh.

"No, I mean, it wouldn't be." Just then, I had a thought. "You know what? Even if there's not another party with people from school, we could have a party of our own—just the four of us. Like a sleepover."

Sara-Beth clapped her hands in delight. "Really, Flan? Just like at the beginning of the summer?"

"Sure. We can do it on Friday." I smiled. "I've been neglecting you guys way too much. I'm sorry."

The rest of the afternoon I spent sprawled up in my room, alternately napping and working on homework. A few days—or even hours—earlier, I might not have believed it, but it actually seemed like I was balancing my two lives really well. I'd gone out with Meredith and Judith, cemented something real with Bennett, and still basically been a good friend to my runaway pals back home. I felt awesome, confident—like I could take over the world. I should've known it was too good to last forever.

Chapter 19

On Monday, I ended up sitting between Meredith and Judith at this lame school assembly that happened in the afternoon. I can't remember what the topic was—something related to students taking a more active role in recycling, or another, even more boring topic—but it didn't really matter, because the three of us stayed entertained the whole time writing notes to one another in the margins of my chemistry notebook. It was like the sleepover all over again: we kept cracking one another up. Fortunately, we were sitting toward the back of the auditorium or else we would have definitely gotten into trouble; as it was, only Mrs. Frisk, one of the librarians, kept turning around and shooting us the evil eye, but other than that, we were on our own.

Flan, have you seen Bennett today? wrote Judith. *I heard he was looking for you before school.*

Crap, I wrote back. *I was blow-drying my hair and got here super late. Oh well. At least he didn't see me with bed-head.*

Not yet! wrote Meredith, giggling.

I elbowed her in the ribs. *What about you? Any cool guy gossip?*

Practically the only guy I've seen today is Principal Leland, wrote Judith, rolling her eyes at the stage, where Principal Leland was standing at the podium, talking into a microphone and sweating under the lights. He's this short, balding guy who wears bow ties and cardigan sweaters with leather patches on the elbows, and even though I think he's sweet, most of the other kids at Stuyvesant find him annoying as hell. *God, wouldn't it be great if he was as cute as that guy from* The United States of Leland? *Or better yet, Leland Brinker?*

Leland Brinker is sooo cute. Meredith underlined the word *so* about a million times. *I'd kill to see him onstage.*

He went out with Sara-Beth Benny for a while, I wrote, deciding to take a chance. After all, it was in all the gossip mags anyway. *He was even at that famous* Survivor *party she threw. They made a cute couple.*

Yeah, right! Judith drew an angry face next to her words. *SBB looks so scary! Someone should make her eat a hamburger or something. She's totally starving herself.*

Maybe she's on coke, Meredith added. *Kills your hunger and explains some of the crazy outfits she wears.*

Leland Brinker could seriously do so much better. What a skank! Judith doodled a cartoon of a stick-figure girl with big sunglasses waving a bikini top in the air. Meredith started giggling hysterically. But I just stared down in my lap while my stomach did guilty flip-flops.

Meredith and Judith weren't mean girls—they'd never say stuff like this about someone they knew. But celebrities just weren't real to them. I was starting to understand why SBB found most of the people in the "real world" so scary: they totally didn't treat her like a person. But I didn't know how to tell Meredith and Judith why their words bothered me so much without giving anything away about Sara-Beth living with me.

I think, I started to write, still trying to figure out how to put it, exactly. But before I could finish my thought, a hand came out of nowhere and closed the notebook. I looked up. It was Mrs. Frisk: Meredith was laughing so hard the old librarian had actually gotten up and come back here to see what was going on.

"Girls," she hissed, "this is an assembly about

Styrofoam disposal—not a social hour. If I see you writing notes again, I'll confiscate them and send all three of you to detention after school." She turned on her heel, went back up several rows, and took her seat again.

Meredith, Judith, and I exchanged glances.

"Rrrear," Judith muttered under her breath, making a claw gesture. I grinned, but I still felt bad about what we'd been writing.

So we pretty much piped down for the rest of the assembly; Mrs. Frisk might be old and persnickety, but that was no reason to get stuck in detention. We sat more or less quietly while Principal Leland did a PowerPoint presentation about the new blue bins they were putting around the school. After what seemed like about three hours, it was finally over.

We were supposed to file out of the auditorium row by row, but everyone was so desperate to get out of there that it wound up being a mad crunch. Meredith, Judith, and I got sort of separated in the aisle, and I was feeling really claustrophobic—until I realized that the guy I was stuck standing next to was none other than Bennett Keating.

"Flan!" He looked like he couldn't be happier to see me. His hair was all tousled and adorable, and he was wearing this khaki jacket that made his shoulders look even broader and stronger than they did normally. "I was looking all over for you earlier!"

"Really?" I blushed. "Well, it's good to see you too."

"Yeah. So, listen, I had such a great time at Devon's party, I was thinking I'd throw one at my dad's apartment this weekend. He's going to be gone on Friday night. Do you think you'd be able to come?"

"Of course," I said, but inside I started to squirm a little. That was the night I was supposed to hang out with the girls at home. "Only, do you think it would be okay if I brought along—"

"Oh yeah, Meredith and Judith are invited too. Where did they go? I just saw them."

I glanced around. "Well, I'll tell them anyway."

"Great. Maybe I'll find you guys in the cafeteria at lunch." Bennett grabbed my hand and gave it a squeeze, then disappeared into the crowd.

Which left me feeling giddy and wonderful, but with just one very disturbing question on my mind: how was I going to explain this one to SBB, Philippa, and Liesel?

My temporary solution wasn't a very good one: I just didn't tell them anything. It was easier than it sounds, because that week all three of them were going crazy, especially SBB, whose realtor had set up an interview with another co-op board late Friday afternoon. Sara-Beth didn't want anything to go wrong this time, so she was in full hide-from-the-paparazzi mode. She even wore her big dark glasses inside the house.

Early in the week, I was able to kid myself into thinking that the girls had forgotten all about our plans to have girl time on Friday night. But then on Thursday, when we were all sitting around the coffee table eating the Thai food we'd ordered for dinner, Philippa said the words I'd been dreading: "So, I've been thinking about our sleepover tomorrow. Should we rent some movies or something?"

"Don't even talk to me about anything Holly-wood." Sara-Beth nibbled at a noodle from her pad Thai. "They chew you up and spit you out. That's how the business works."

"One of my friends from Cube works for the Sundance Channel," Liesel offered. "He could get us some films that haven't been released yet. Or we could do each other's nails. There's this wonderful store that just opened, and they sell the most unusual colors—"

"Let's hear it, Flan." Philippa turned to me. "You're the sleepover expert. What do you think would be the most fun?"

I swallowed a mouthful of my green curry, but it didn't go down easily.

"Listen," I said, "do you think we could do this sleepover thing another night? Like . . . Saturday?"

All three of them looked at me like I'd just fallen in through the ceiling. I hunched over my food and continued, "I mean, it's just that . . . I have this other thing I'm supposed to do."

Total silence. Liesel was the first to speak, and when she did, she sounded horrified, like this was a nightmare beyond her worst imaginings.

"You . . . double-booked?" she whispered. "You double-booked . . . us?"

"I didn't mean to," I said, feeling pretty awful. "I

mean, seriously, I didn't. But then, the other day, Bennett said there was going to be another party—"

"Another party?" Sara-Beth shrieked. "But Flan, you promised you'd bring us along next time."

"I know . . . but . . . I didn't want to tell you about it, because, well, because . . ." I had to think fast, but I just kept picturing Meredith and Judith and how shocked they'd look if I showed up at the party with three older girls they'd never seen or even heard about before—including SBB. "Because I know you have that board meeting on Friday. What if it goes really well, and then you turn around and get your picture snapped when we're out that night? You'd lose the apartment, and all for the sake of some dumb Stuyvesant party? I don't think so."

Sara-Beth still looked hurt. She crossed her arms over her chest.

"That's no reason why we can't go, though," said Philippa. "Liesel and me, I mean."

"Yeah, but I don't know. It's not going to be anything great. I mean, they might play spin-the-bottle, but it's the beginning of flu season, you know. So I bet it'll mostly be other stuff . . . like Yahtzee." I tried to think of all the lamest stuff I could imagine. "And I think Bennett said there were going to be charades. Yeah, loads of charades."

"If this party's so dumb, why are you going?" Sara-Beth didn't wait for me to answer. She got up and went up the stairs.

"Sara-Beth," I called after her. Philippa and Liesel exchanged a look. I could tell they were totally disgusted with me.

"Well, I suppose we can amuse ourselves," Liesel said to me, really coldly.

"Yeah. Besides, we shouldn't leave Sara-Beth trapped at home all alone," said Philippa pointedly. "That would be really mean."

I'd pretty much never felt worse—that is, until I went upstairs and found Sara-Beth curled up on my bed, holding my teddy bear to her face and crying her eyes out. Noodles was nuzzling into her neck, then panting and looking concerned. At that point, I would have gladly changed places with anyone in the world. But since that wasn't an option, I went and perched on the edge of the bed until Sara-Beth finally rolled over and looked up at me with big red accusing eyes.

"I'm sorry," I said. "I didn't mean to make you feel left out."

SBB sniffled. "I don't hate you, Flan. Don't think that I do. I just don't understand how you can be so cruel to me."

"Sara-Beth, that's really not fair. I'm not doing this

to hurt you. I'd take you with me if I could." At that moment, it really was almost true. I would have done anything to stop her from crying. I pulled Noodles over onto my lap, and he started licking my hands. "But you said yourself, you can't go out to parties. The paparazzi would see you, and then you'd never get in the co-op. It sucks, but I mean, that's the way it is, right?"

"You just don't understand," she wept. "I'd give anything to just be normal. Like you."

I blinked. Me, normal? "What do you mean?"

"I can't make any friends. . . . I'm always hiding out . . . and now you're running away from me! I'm going to end up all alone, just like that mean old gypsy said!" She wiped her nose on my bedspread. "Oh, Flan, wouldn't it be perfect if we were sisters? Then we could do each other's hair . . . and stay up all night talking . . . and go to each other's graduations . . . and do all the wonderful things that sisters get to do!"

"But we can do all of that already," I said. A little calmer now, Noodles jumped down from my lap onto the floor. "We stayed up all night talking, like, three days ago."

"Oh, Flanny, do you mean it?" Suddenly, Sara-Beth perked up. She looked at me intently. "You're not just saying it?"

"Umm . . . saying what?"

"You really think of me as a sister already?"

"Sara-Beth, do you have any brothers and sisters?" I asked.

"Well, on *Mike's Princesses*—"

"No, but *real* brothers and sisters. Ones you're actually related to."

She shook her head.

I got up and grabbed a box of Kleenex from on top of my dresser. "Well, I think maybe that's why you have this . . . weird idea of what siblings are like. I mean, it's not like sisters are best friends all the time."

"They're not?"

"No. My sister February is six years older than me. When we were growing up, we hardly ever played together." I handed her the tissue box. "Sometimes she'd dress me up and put makeup on me like I was her little doll, but that was about it. Most of the time I'd just do stupid stuff, like drool on her new shirt or break her lipstick, and she'd yell at me."

"But we wouldn't be like that. You're hardly three years younger than me. And you don't drool any-more. At least I don't think you do."

"Yeah, but we'd still fight. The reason you and me are such good friends now is that we have, I dunno, a little distance from each other. Like, you can leave anytime you want. We never feel trapped together. If we were on one of the family vacations I took as a kid, where we'd be on my parents' sailboat for, like, four weeks straight, you can bet we'd start getting annoyed with each other. Maybe even majorly annoyed."

Sara-Beth was silent. She plucked at the pillowcase thoughtfully. "I never thought about it like that."

"But it's totally true. I think the best friends are people who spend a lot of time together but then get to be apart too. That helps make the times they're together more special."

Sara-Beth nodded.

"Flan?" she asked finally. "Do you really think we're best friends now?"

"Sure I do," I said, and the minute the words were out of my mouth, I realized they were true. "You know me better than anybody else, Sara-Beth."

"And you really think we need . . . space . . . to stay best friends?"

"I dunno. It's just something to think about." Reaching down to pet Noodles, I snuck a glance over at Sara-Beth. I couldn't tell if my words had really sunk in, but I could tell she hadn't totally tuned me out either. She looked serious, but she wasn't crying or anything, so that seemed like a good sign. "Listen, if you really want me to stay home tomorrow night I will. I never thought my going out would upset everybody so much."

Sara-Beth blew her nose loudly. "No. You should go, Flan. You're right—I don't want to make you feel trapped."

"Are you sure it's okay?"

"Yeah. But on one condition: I want all the details."

"Of course." I reached over to give SBB a hug. It was sort of awkward, but good. Still, this whole disaster had taught me a lesson: I needed to be much, much more careful with my friends' feelings.

Chapter 21

$\mathcal{O}$n Friday, I went straight to Meredith's apartment after school to get ready for the party. She and Judith and I were all really excited—two parties in two weeks! How cool could we get? We all got dressed—I borrowed this denim miniskirt of Meredith's with a beaded rose appliqué—and then we went out for pizza together and made our way over to Bennett's apartment, which was on the Upper West Side.

I'd never been to his building before, so I was psyched to see where he lived. The Upper West Side is nice, but it can be kind of boring sometimes, with crummy French bistros about every two blocks and a lot of old people pushing around those weird little shopping carts that they use for their groceries or medications or whatever. But the bagels are good and there are some nice bookstores up there, so I don't mind it too much.

Bennett lived up near Riverside Park, and his building kind of looked like a cake: it was white and tall and square, with complicated decorations up along the top. We went in, took the elevator up to the sixth floor, and walked to the apartment.

"Hey, you're here!" said Bennett, letting us in. He gave me a big hug, and I grinned. This was going to be the best party ever.

So far, there weren't that many people there; maybe ten sophomores, including Jules and Eric, were scattered around the living room, drinking punch out of plastic cups and listening to the All-American Rejects album playing on the stereo. Two boys were in front of the TV playing an X-Men video game. The apartment itself was nice—dark wood paneling on the walls, a fireplace, and a view of Riverside Park out the windows—but it looked like it'd been decorated by someone with boxing gloves and a blindfold on. A pullout sofa, a pair of beanbag chairs, and a wagon-wheel coffee table were the main furniture in the living room, and a poster for the movie *L.A. Confidential* hung prominently on one wall.

"So, you live here with your dad?" I asked Bennett as I looked around.

He shrugged. "Yeah, on weekends mostly. The rest of the time I'm with my mom—she lives downtown—

but I could never have a party there. She notices when one little thing is out of place."

Meredith and Judith went to get some punch, and I sat down with Bennett on the pullout sofa. I leaned against his shoulder. The longer I was in the apartment, the less the tackiness bothered me.

"How've you been?" he asked. "I feel like we've barely gotten a chance to talk all week."

"All right. Mostly just stressed out." It seemed really wrong, somehow, that he was showing me his home and I still hadn't told him practically anything about my life, but I didn't even know where to start. "There's just way too much drama at my house, you know?"

"Yeah? Man, you should see my folks when they're fighting. It's a nightmare." Bennett shook his head. "If they hadn't gotten divorced, I seriously think they would've exploded my eardrums by now."

"Well, I'm glad I'm here now."

He smiled, showing his chipped tooth. "Me too."

The whole time Bennett and I were sitting in the corner talking, the room was filling up with people. Apparently some of the older kids had showed up fashionably late after all. It started getting a little wild, and definitely hot and loud, with the music turned up and people dancing, or sort of standing around in groups together, moving their shoulders to the music, like they were too cool to actually dance. After a while, I realized I hadn't seen Judith and Meredith for a long time, and even though I really wanted to stay there talking to Bennett, I realized they might feel like I'd ditched them for a guy if we didn't go looking for them soon. And that would suck.

"Where do you think they went?" Bennett asked as we got up to start looking around.

"I dunno." I stood on my tiptoes, but even though I'm kind of tall, it was hard to see much of anything in a room so filled with people. "Should we look in the kitchen? Maybe they went to get more punch."

"Let's hold hands." Bennett coughed. "I mean, we don't want to get separated."

"Okay." I took his hand. Could this evening be going any better?

After a lot of pushing, we finally got to a space in the room where we could breathe without bumping into someone. I stood on my tiptoes again to look around.

"There they are," I said, tugging on Bennett's hand. Meredith and Judith were over by the entrance to the kitchen, holding cups of punch and looking around. They seemed to have gotten shoved around by the party too: Meredith had a run in her tights, and

Judith had spilled punch on her tank top. "We should go over to them."

"Looks like they're coming over here." Bennett pointed with his free hand. Meredith had spotted us and was waving like we were the best thing that had happened to them all night.

Just then, someone tapped me on the shoulder. And it wasn't one of my friends.

"Hey, I know you," said this guy. He was wearing a white T-shirt with Hugo Boss suit pants and flip-flops, and he looked older—eleventh grade, maybe. He had his hair slicked back and his skin was really pink, like he'd just gotten a facial. Bennett looked at me questioningly, but I didn't know what to say. The guy was sort of familiar, but I didn't really recognize him.

"Sorry, you must be thinking of somebody else," I said.

"No, I'm positive. Man, why can't I remember?"

"Hey, Bennett," said Judith, pushing through the crowd. "Great party. Hey, Flan."

"Flan!" The Hugo Boss guy clapped his hands together like he'd just discovered a new planet or something. "Flan Flood! Of course. You're Patch Flood's little sister."

"Oh. Yeah, I guess, um—" Bennett and I were still holding hands, but our palms were getting sweaty. I glanced at Meredith and Judith. They both looked really curious.

"Don't you remember me? We met at that club, whatsitsname, Lotus. You were there with your brother and that guy Jonathan, and David and Mickey Pardo kept throwing cake at some other people I was with and it turned into kind of a riot. I'm Harrison Grand Williams the Third."

Now I remembered. That night in Lotus had been my fourteenth birthday, and a bunch of us were just hanging out since my real party had gone haywire. Harrison had come over to our table to talk to my brother, who he claimed to know from private school, and he'd been totally annoying, gossiping about random people and trying to act like he was one of my brother's friends, the Insiders, which he was so not. SBB had been there that night too—she was the one who got me into the club—but apparently she'd been pretty well disguised, because if Harrison had recognized her, he totally would have been sucking up to her too.

"Oh yeah," I said. Right now I was starting to wish *I* had a disguise on. "Harrison."

"How's Patch? Still throwing those wild parties? That last one was a riot. When that male stripper showed up and started rapping, I thought I'd die laughing."

Meredith, Judith, and Bennett were all really staring

at me now. I felt like I was onstage and I didn't know my lines.

"I wasn't at that one," I lied.

"Oh, come on. I'm sure you were. Don't you remember? Or maybe I'm just thinking of that other party—Liesel Reid's sweet sixteen. I'm sure I saw you there. You know, with the pink champagne? Where Mickey Pardo stole the horse? I know you were at that one, because I remember someone saying, 'Hey, there's Patch Flood's little sister. And who's that girl with her? Is that Sara-Beth Benny?'"

The whole room was getting quieter now, and Harrison's voice was getting louder; with the mention of SBB's name, several people turned to stare at us. I wanted to fall through the floor. That party had been in every gossip column in the city.

"I guess this party's a little tame by your standards, huh?" Harrison glanced around appraisingly. "Who's even throwing this thing?"

"Um," I said.

Meredith and Judith were staring at me like I'd just confirmed all their worst suspicions. And then Bennett's hand slipped out of mine. His face was burning red.

"Bennett, wait!" I yelled.

But he was shouldering his way into the crowd, away from me.

*T*he cab ride back home was really silent and tense. I sat in the middle, with Meredith and Judith on either side of me, and they both looked out the window the whole time. I don't think I've ever felt so ignored in my whole life. We were supposed to go to Judith's to sleep over again, but about halfway there, I told the driver to drop them off first and then take me back to Perry Street. The girls didn't protest.

"Listen," I said after a long, long silence. "I'm really . . . sorry."

Judith and Meredith looked at each other—it was like they were having a conversation with their eyes.

"I just don't get it, Flan," said Judith. Outside the window, closed-up shops swirled by. "Who are you, seriously? I thought we were friends."

"We *are* friends, Judith."

"Then why didn't you tell us any of that stuff?"

asked Meredith. "I mean, your parties, your brother—who, by the way, is totally famous—everyone at our grade school used to read that anonymous blog that chronicled his every move—it's like you're hiding us from all the cool people in your life."

"I'm not hiding you guys," I said. "I'm just—"

"Then explain to me why you won't have us over to your house." Judith turned back to the window angrily.

My cell phone made the little musical sound that it does when I get a text. I flipped it open and found the longest message I'd ever received:

OH MY GOD FLAN THE BOARD IS TOTALLY PSYCHO THEY TRIED TO PRY INTO MY PERSONAL LIFE BUT I WOULDN'T HAVE IT OF COURSE AND THEY FREAKED OUT AND TOLD ME THAT IF I DIDN'T STOP SOBBING THEY'D HAVE TO CALL AN AMBULANCE AND I WAS LIKE IF I WANT TO SOB I'LL SOB I'M A BIG STAR AND HOW COULD YOU FORSAKE ME IN MY HOUR OF NEED FLAN I THINK I'M GOING TO STAY AT YOUR PLACE A FEW MORE DAYS BUT AT THE SAME TIME YOU DIDN'T DO ANYTHING TO STOP THIS FROM HAPPENING YOU DIDN'T EVEN COME HOME AFTER SCHOOL TODAY AND I NEEDED YOU TO

QUIZ ME AND HELP ME PREPARE AND PICK OUT CLOTHES FOR ME TO WEAR AND ALSO YOU SAID BEFORE YOU'D WRITE ME A RECOMMENDATION WHICH YOU NEVER DID BUT ANYWAY I JUST THOUGHT YOU SHOULD KNOW THAT MICKEY AND PHILIPPA HAVE MADE YOUR SISTER'S ATTIC INTO A LITTLE LOVE NEST AND WHENEVER THEY COME DOWNSTAIRS THEY'RE EITHER ARGUING OR TALKING GROSS BABY TALK AND ALWAYS WITH THE PDA AND I WAS ALL LIKE GET A ROOM AND THEY WERE LIKE WE ALREADY HAVE A WHOLE FLOOR AND I WAS LIKE GET A ROOM OUTSIDE OF MY HOUSE YOU HORRIBLE HORRIBLE PEOPLE AND THEY WERE ALL LIKE THIS ISN'T YOUR HOUSE AND MEANWHILE LIESEL IS BEING SUCH A TOTAL BITCH AND SHE'S WEARING A HEADSET NOW CAUSE SHE'S ON THE PHONE SO MUCH AND NOODLES CHEWED UP HER SHOES SO OF COURSE SHE THREW A TOTAL FIT AND I TOLD HER IF SHE CAN'T DEAL SHE SHOULD JUST LEAVE TOO AND THEN SHE

I stopped reading and shut my phone. It was really disturbing to think of SBB crying and typing into the tiny pad of her cell phone across town, and I just couldn't handle it right then. I couldn't even solve my own problems, let alone hers.

"Things are just really complicated right now." I looked over at Meredith, but she averted her eyes. "You've got to believe me. I'm not ashamed of you guys."

"I'll bet," Judith snorted.

My phone made another little sound and against my better judgment I opened it again.

FLAN YOU NEED TO COME HOME RIGHT NOW SBB IS ACTING REALLY UNSTABLE AND SHE'S THREATENING MICKEY WITH HER AIR HORN

"Who keeps texting you?" Judith demanded.

"This old friend of mine is kind of messed up. But listen, I'm not going to deal with her right now. It doesn't matter."

"See? That's a perfect example of what I'm talking about. What's happening with you *does* matter. But you won't tell us anything—you won't let us meet any of your other friends, or invite us to any of your parties. You're totally ashamed of us, and I can't take it anymore. I won't."

"I don't see why you guys are so mad. It's not like any of this was top secret or anything. If you'd asked me, I wouldn't have lied. It's not like it takes a genius to recognize my last name."

"Yeah, well, somehow I assumed that if you had a brother, especially one who's basically world famous for blowing off the title of Hottest Private School Boy, you would have brought him up by now!" Judith was getting really mad—a strand of her hair had come loose and she kept puffing to keep it out of her eyes.

"Listen," I said, "my brother is just one little tiny thing about my life, so I don't see why I should be talking about him all the time. But even if I didn't mention him on purpose, that doesn't mean I don't like you. I'm here, aren't I? Why would I hang out with you if I'm so embarrassed to be your friend?"

"Oh, I don't know. Maybe you tell all of your celebrity buddies about us and sit around laughing all day. I mean, you're probably laughing at us right now! How lame we are, leaving a party at eleven without even getting kissed."

"Or talking to a boy, practically," Meredith murmured sadly.

I shook my head. "You've got this all wrong. Most of the time I just sit at home watching movies by myself. The only reason I know any of those people Harrison mentioned is because of my brother. Patch is the cool one, not me. And even if I were cool, I'd never make fun of you, not in a million years. You guys have been nicer to me than anybody else at Stuyvesant."

Judith and Meredith exchanged doubtful glances. After a long moment, Meredith spoke.

"I really like you, Flan," Meredith said softly. "It's just, our old school was filled with, well, bitches. They'd be nice to your face, and then the minute you were gone they'd double-cross you. It was awful. Judith and I were the only ones who could trust each other, because we've been friends since forever. We talked it over and decided we needed a change. So we came to Stuyvesant to get away from all that."

Judith nodded. "Unless you can show us you're not two-faced, we just can't keep hanging out with you. I'm sick of feeling stupid all the time. Seriously."

The cab pulled up to their street, and Meredith and Judith got out—leaving me in the backseat all by myself. Traffic was slowed to a crawl, the cab hit every red light, and it was a long, long ride back home to Perry Street. I felt completely miserable, and it seemed like this night could not possibly get any worse.

When the cab pulled up in front of my house, I saw Mickey getting ready to leave on his Vespa. I opened the door to wave to him, but before I could get his attention, he gunned the engine and took off down the street. He certainly was in a hurry to get away from whatever was going on in my house. I took a deep breath, paid the driver, and went inside.

I knew it was going to be bad, but nothing could have prepared me for what I saw. Couch cushions lay scattered around the floor, some with holes ripped in them, like leftovers from a particular angry pillow fight, and someone had ground rice crisps into the carpet with the sole of her shoe. Noodles had apparently forgotten whatever housebreaking he'd learned in his last home, because he'd made messes all over the place. Designer dresses lay on the furniture, like crumpled ghost-sheets, and empty soda bottles, wine bottles, and prescription pill bottles for SBB's various medications were all over the floor, lying on their sides. And that was just the living room! I didn't want to imagine what I might find upstairs. Never, not even after one of Patch's crazy parties, had I seen the place in such terrible shape.

I didn't know what to do. My first thought was to call my parents and confess everything: "Hey, I know I was supposed to be starting high school and concentrating on my homework, but guess what? I invited three of my friends to move in with us, and they trashed everything!" But something stopped me: maybe the possibility (unlikely) that my folks would freak out, hurry home, and kick my butt—or maybe the possibility (more likely) that they'd be mad but say it was my responsibility and leave me to fix it on my own anyway. So I kept my cell phone in my pocket. Instead I pulled off my shoes and yelled, "Philippa? Liesel? Sara-Beth? You guys around here anywhere?"

They appeared, all together, at the top of the stairs. They didn't look happy, but at least they weren't yelling or clawing one another's eyes out, so I took that to be a good sign.

"What happened?" I asked, gesturing at the huge mess. "It looks like a mosh pit or something in here.

This isn't cool, you guys, seriously. I'm sorry I left you all alone, but I've had a really hard night."

But none of them said anything. They all just stared at me, and I started to realize why they weren't fighting anymore. They were united now. Against me.

"Listen," I went on, "I'm really sorry I ditched you guys to go to that party. Believe me, I wish I'd just stayed home. I had an awful time. From now on, I promise I won't go off and not invite you guys. It was mean and stupid and wrong of me. Okay? I'm really sorry. Beyond sorry. What else do you want me to say?"

Philippa held up my chemistry notebook. "Maybe you could explain this."

For a second, I didn't know what she was talking about. Then I realized she had it open to the page where Judith, Meredith, and I had been scribbling notes to one another during the school assembly. And right in the middle of the page was the picture Judith had drawn of stick-figure SBB stripping.

"How could you say those things about me, Flan?" wept Sara-Beth. "I thought you were my friend."

"It's one thing to . . . double-book us, Flan," said Liesel, "but it's another to turn against someone who trusts you."

"But wait, I didn't write those things. Judith—"

"Sure, blame it all on somebody else," scoffed Philippa. "That's so mature."

"But I really didn't—"

"I know when I'm not wanted." Sara-Beth wiped her eyes. "Tonight you can rest easy knowing you'll never see me again. I don't care if I am homeless—I'm not going to spend one more hour in this horrible, horrible house!"

"Sara-Beth, wait!" But before I could get my shoes back on, she was running down the stairs, past me, out the front door, and out into the street. I chased her out onto the sidewalk, but she was already disappearing into a cab. "Wait!" I yelled. But she didn't so much as say good-bye.

Now I felt really sick. I went back inside the house. Liesel and Philippa were sitting on the couch now, their arms crossed, their faces as stony as a pair of judges'. I didn't look at them as I ran up the stairs to my bedroom, shut the door, and locked it.

As soon as I crashed down onto my bed, Noodles came out from under it. He hopped up next to me and started licking my face. But, as cute as he was, even he made me sad, because he reminded me of Liesel and Sara-Beth and how much fun we'd had hanging out at Cube the night I got him. I hugged the little doggy to my chest and started to cry. Everyone hated me: my friends from home, my friends from school, the guy I liked—everybody. I'd humiliated Bennett in his own house, made Judith and Meredith not trust me—and worst of all, SBB thought I'd basically called her an anorexic prostitute. It was awful and ugly and stupid, and I wanted to die.

After several hours of crying and hating myself, I finally fell asleep. All night long I had a series of terrifying dreams, filled with people yelling at me and sentencing me to jail. But when I woke up the next morning, the voices I heard in real life were even more terrifying. They belonged to my parents, and they were coming from downstairs.

Chapter 24

QUALITY TIME WITH THE FOLKS

I got dressed in a hurry, then crept down the stairs, trying to make as little noise as possible; maybe I could sneak out of the house before the fireworks started. My parents are gone a lot, sure, but when my dad gets back from traveling he sometimes gets randomly strict and expects everything to be a certain way, like he's making up for all the time we were completely unsupervised. Patch and Feb and I will be like, "Whatever, when you guys were in Southeast Asia we did what we wanted and everything was cool." And sometimes there's an argument, but my mom hates fighting, so it usually settles down pretty quickly. This time, though, I knew even she wouldn't be on my side—and I didn't want to find out what would happen then.

When I got to the bottom of the stairs, though, I couldn't believe my eyes. The living room was immaculate. All the cushions were back on the sofa, the floor had been vacuumed, the pictures were straight on the walls, the lightbulb in the lamp had been replaced. Someone had even taken the time to dust the screen of the TV and put the remotes and video game controllers back where they belonged. What's more, there was no sign of Philippa, Liesel, or SBB anywhere—not so much as a suitcase or a high-heeled shoe. It was like elves had come in the night and set everything right—only, somehow, seeing everything all in place like this made me feel even worse. It was like one of those awful fairy tales where someone gets her wish and spends the rest of her life wishing she hadn't.

I went into the kitchen and found my parents. Earlier, I think I said good looks run in the Flood family. Well, my folks are so beautiful that sometimes it's hard to believe they're parents and not just pictures cut out of a magazine. My mother is tall and kind of willowy, with ash-blond hair and a faraway smile that never quite comes into focus, like the fuzzy lenses they used to use on movie actresses back in the forties. She has the best posture of anyone I've ever seen—back in college, she used to think she wanted to be a dancer, but I guess she just lost interest after she married my dad and discovered the perks and pleasures of a life of nonstop world travel. Plus, she had three kids, which probably puts you out of commission for dancing, at least for a little while.

She loves being a mom too; when we were little, she spoiled us all rotten, and there's still nothing I like better than when she takes me shopping. Today she had on a pair of Versace jeans and an old burnt-umber cashmere sweater of my dad's. She'd kicked off her shoes, these sandal-y heels with a bunch of inter-woven straps, but the way she'd left them on the floor, they looked more elegant than they would on most people's feet.

I probably look more like my dad, who's also blond, but in a more sunshiny kind of way. He plays a lot of tennis, so he's always tan, which just makes his huge smile seem even brighter. When I was little, I used to think he looked like Guy Smiley from *Sesame Street*, but now I think he's more like Dennis Quaid. Right now, he was sitting at the table, doing the *Times* crossword. He was so intent on it that he barely noticed me come in, but my mom, who was peering into the refrigerator, turned around with a big smile and clapped her hands together.

"Flan, honey! We've missed you so much."

"What are you guys doing here?" I asked, coming over to give her a hug. My dad set down his pen.

"Don't look so glad to see us," he said, getting up.

"I'm sorry. I'm just surprised. I thought you guys were going to Marrakech." I gave him a hug too, then sat down at the table. "Uh, and I'm not sure we had a chance to clean up—"

"We were about to leave, but on the way to the airport, we decided that maybe we should be around for our baby's first year of high school. So we turned the car around and drove straight into the city." My dad grinned. "Of course, we called and had the cleaning service in before we arrived—you know how your mother hates to come home to a messy house. Anyway, look at you, so grown-up! I hope your brother and sister have been taking good care of you."

"Um . . . yeah."

"Where are they, sweetie?" asked my mom, taking a bag of oranges out of a drawer in the fridge. "They really shouldn't leave you home alone like this."

"I think Patch had to be somewhere . . . early this morning. Besides, I can take care of myself okay," I added defensively. If they only knew. "Is it okay if I go check my e-mail?"

"Don't take too long," said my dad. "We're making breakfast. Thought you kids could use a home-cooked meal for a change."

"Sure." Forcing a smile, I walked out into the living

room, wondering how I'd explain that I hadn't seen my brother or sister for weeks. But before I could get too worried, I spotted Patch, slouched on the sofa in an old DEFEND BROOKLYN T-shirt and jeans, eating a croissant.

"Mom! Dad! Patch's back!" I called, trying to hide the delight in my voice.

My mom appeared in the doorway to the kitchen, holding a spatula. "Oh, good. Honey, don't spoil your appetite. We're making omelets."

"'Kay," said Patch, finishing the croissant and licking his fingers. My mom went back into the kitchen.

"Where have you been?" I whispered as soon as she was out of earshot. "I thought I was going to have some serious explaining to do."

"I've been staying with some friends. You know—chilling." He settled back on the cushions. "I met this girl. She's pretty awesome. The only problem is, her fiancé's this French diplomat and they're going back—"

I shook my head. "Listen, Patch, I'm really sorry if you're going through a hard time. But seriously, I have enough problems of my own right now." The minute I said it, I felt really bad. What was I turning into? Queen Bitch?

Patch whistled. "Whoa. Sorry."

"Wait, I shouldn't have said that. It's just, things've been crazy since you left. You have no idea. I've made such a mess of everything. My friends . . . this guy . . ." Suddenly I felt like I might start crying. Patch scooted over on the couch and I plopped down next to him, covering my face with my hands.

"Hey, hey, be cool. I understand." Patch ruffled my hair sympathetically. "It's easy for me to forget you're growing up sometimes. I still just think of you as my kid sister, you know? But you've got your own life. That's the way things should be." He scrutinized me. "You want to tell me what's going on?"

"Ugh, no," I said. "I don't want to get into it all right now. It's just something I have to figure out. But thanks for asking—really. It's good knowing I have someone I can talk to." It wasn't every day that my big brother treated me like one of his friends. I thought about how much had changed since he drove me to Connecticut at the beginning of the summer. He was right: it was easy to forget sometimes, but I really was growing up. And doing a pretty lousy job of it too. "I wish I was more like you, Patch. You're so good at making friends."

"But don't you get it, Flan? You don't want to be like me, or anybody else. The only way to get along with people is by being yourself. It's a cliché, I know, but it's also a good way to avoid a lot of bull." He folded his arms behind his head. "Listen, I don't know what's been going on with you, but I'd hazard a guess that if you just open up to people, let them see who you really are, a lot of these so-called problems'll disappear. Because people like you, sis, they really do—but what they like about you is that you're real."

I nodded. He was right, and I had so not been doing that. But now I was starting to get an idea of how to fix the situation.

While my parents made omelets and juiced oranges in the new high-tech juicer they'd bought, I went back upstairs to my bedroom. I sat down at my desk and took out my stationery—the pale yellow monogrammed stuff I hardly ever use—and carefully started to write. As I wrote names on the envelopes, I thought about what it was I really wanted. Because I used to think I wanted to be normal, just a regular teenager like everybody else. But now I was beginning to realize it was more complicated than that. I didn't want to blend in—I wanted to stand out. Not for knowing celebrities or all the best clubs, not for who my brother was or for how much money my parents had. No, I wanted to stand out by being me. The real me—Flan Flood.

Chapter 25

On Monday, I got to school way early and started combing the halls for Meredith and Judith, and it was a good thing I did, because they were practically impossible to find. They weren't at Meredith's locker, or Judith's; they weren't in the hall outside our first-period class, and they weren't by the cafeteria. Finally I found them hiding out by the sixth-floor escalator. I kind of had a feeling that they were avoiding me, but I tried to tell myself I was just being paranoid.

"Hey," I said. "I've been looking all over for you guys. What are you doing up here?"

Meredith and Judith stopped their conversation abruptly and turned around. They looked at me warily, like they were trying to decide if I was going to bite them or not. Meredith was wearing a vintage T-shirt with a screen print of Jim Morrison on it, but Judith

174

was all dressed up in a suit and heels like she was about to go work in an office or something.

"I'm trying out for the debate team," Judith said finally. "I was supposed to be up here for that. But they pushed back my audition till after school."

"That's cool."

"Not really. Now I have to walk around in a suit all day, or change into normal clothes and then change back." She looked at her watch. "Which I don't have time to do before first period."

"Well, I think you look nice," Meredith told her.

"Me too," I said.

Judith grudgingly smiled. "Did you have a fun weekend?" she asked, but in this way that made me feel like she was suspicious or something. "Worn out from partying?"

"The only party I went to was with you guys." I looked down at my feet. It was so unfair—how could they think I was out having fun when I was really just sitting around the house, crying and feeling miserable because I thought they hated my guts? Then again, they had no way of knowing how I really felt. "Besides that, I mostly just did homework."

"Us too," said Meredith. "It was super boring."

"Yeah, it was," I agreed.

"Well, next time you're 'bored,' you can ask us to

come over and study with you," said Judith. "But somehow I doubt that'll ever happen."

It was mean, but I deserved it. We all stood there awkwardly for a second, until finally, I took a deep breath and took out the invitations I'd made that weekend.

"Actually," I said in a small voice, "I was wondering if you guys had any plans for Friday."

"This Friday?" asked Judith, the skepticism leaving her voice. She tugged on the sleeves of her suit. "Why do you ask?"

I handed them the invitations that I'd written out so carefully on my stationery. I hoped I wasn't wasting it: my grandma'd had it made for me back when I was twelve, and I'd been rationing it out ever since.

"Yeah. I was thinking about having a little get-together," I said. "You know, like a party. At my house. Since I haven't had you guys over yet."

"A party?" asked Meredith.

"At your house?" asked Judith.

"Yeah. I mean, it's just going to be small—you guys and a couple of my other girlfriends. I was thinking about inviting Bennett, Eric, and Jules too, if that seems like a good idea to you. But you'd get to meet my family—see my real life. Does that sound okay?"

Meredith grinned, and it was like one of those days

when it's cloudy and you can't tell if it's going to rain until the sun finally breaks through. I could tell she'd wanted to trust me all along, and that thought made me feel way, way better.

"See, Judith?" she said. "I told you she wasn't like the others. She does like us."

"Of course I do," I put in quickly. "You guys are amazing. I'm just sorry I wasn't more honest with you from the start."

Judith nodded slowly. I could see there was still a little bit of doubt lurking in her face. "So, should we . . . bring anything?"

"No, no, just yourselves. But you think you'll be able to make it?"

"Sure." Meredith nodded. "We wouldn't miss it for the world."

Now I just had to invite Bennett and the guys. I thought it would be easier after I'd talked to Meredith and Judith, but their reaction hadn't made me feel as confident as I would've liked. Not that I blamed them: you can't just go from being a total phony to winning back someone's trust by handing out an invitation. But I wished they had at least invited me to hang out after school or something. By the end of the day, I just wanted to go home, curl up on the couch, and watch

Breakfast at Tiffany's. Somehow that movie always cheers me up when I feel lousy.

I knew I couldn't, though, so as soon as the last bell rang, I went looking for Bennett. But finding him after school was almost as hard as finding Judith and Meredith before school had been. After I checked the hallway with his locker and the journalism room, I was about to give up and assume he'd already gone home. But going down the last escalator to the first floor, I saw he was standing over by the entrance, talking to some of his friends.

I felt nervous, especially because he was talking to people I didn't know. But it looked like they were saying good-bye—they were all doing those sort of silly complicated handshakes guys always do, and a couple of them were already out the door—and besides, it was now or never. So I walked over to Bennett and, as casually as I could, reached up and tapped him on the shoulder.

"H-hey, Bennett," I stammered as he turned around.

"See you guys," he called to his friends. Then he picked up his backpack and slung it onto his shoulder, and we started walking out of the building together. "Flan," he said, sort of casual, but also sort of cold. "What's up?"

"Not much. Listen, I just wanted to ask you something." I stopped walking, and so did he. There we were, on the sidewalk in front of the school, with all these other students milling around us.

"Well, ask me, then."

For a second, I felt tongue-tied, but I knew that if I just stood there like an idiot, staring at him, I'd just feel even more stupid. So I blurted it out as fast as I could: "I'm having a party on Friday, and I was wondering if you'd like to come."

"Huh. Well, Friday . . . yeah, Friday, I think . . ." Bennett's voice was all hesitant, like he wasn't sure he could be bothered, and it annoyed me a little. Didn't he know how hard this was for me?

I took the invitation out of my backpack and handed it to him. "All the information's on here."

"Cool." Bennett folded the invitation and put it into his pocket. But something was still wrong. Maybe he wasn't trying to act cool after all. He had this weird look on his face like he was nervous but didn't want to show it. "Well, I'll see if I can make it. Have a nice afternoon."

"What's wrong?" I asked, trying to keep up with him. He was walking really fast all of a sudden, as if he was trying to get away from me.

"Listen, I don't want your pity, okay?" he said,

gazing out at the taxis passing us on the street. "If you like me, then like me—but if you feel sorry for me, with my lame-o parties and my dumb comic books—"

"Bennett, what are you talking about?"

"Listen, I'm not stupid, okay?" He kicked a little rock with his sneaker. "If I'd known you were the queen of the scene, I wouldn't have tried to impress you with such a stupid little party."

I blinked. "You threw that party—to make me like you?"

"Well, you had such a good time at Devon's . . . I just thought . . . Oh, forget it." Bennett jammed his hands in his pockets. He tried to say something, but a bus roaring by drowned out his words, and he waved his hand like it didn't matter anyway. But before he could start walking again, I grabbed on to his sleeve.

"Listen," I told him, "I loved the party you threw. It was the best."

"Yeah right." He snorted. "I've heard about parties at the Flood house. Celebrities, bottles of Cristal, all kinds of awesome crazy stuff. I'm not sure drinking ginger ale on my couch really lives up to all that."

I'd never felt more exasperated in my life. "Bennett, those are my brother's parties you've heard about. I've never even had a party with boys at it before."

He squinted at me like he wasn't sure whether to trust me or not. "Really?"

"Yeah. And I'm sorry if it's disappointing or whatever, but I'm only inviting, like, ten people to the one on Friday."

A pair of girls in dance leotards walked toward us, and Bennett stepped to my side of the sidewalk to let them pass. When they were gone, he asked, "Why?"

"Because I don't like all that over-the-top stuff. I just want to spend time with . . . with the people I really care about."

Bennett half-smiled, showing his chipped front tooth, and we started walking together again.

"How's everything with the school paper?" I asked.

"Oh, that's not very exciting. You don't want to hear about that."

"Of course I do."

"Huh." He ran his hand through his hair. "Well, I guess there was a big stink about the gossip column this week. We printed something about how Principal Leland's been going out with the girls' volleyball coach."

"Principal Leland?" I laughed. "But that guy's so old and creepy!"

"That's what the volleyball coach said too. She was pretty mad—called it slander. And Principal Leland was like, 'Oh, give them some allowances, they're just children,' but you could tell he loved reading that he was hooking up with this athletic younger chick." Bennett shook his head. "Man, oh man."

"That's so funny, Bennett," I told him.

"Yeah, I guess the paper can be pretty entertaining. I dunno, for us dorks who work on it anyway."

"Stop saying that. You're not a dork."

And then something wonderful happened. We were stepping off the curb, over a puddle, when out of nowhere, a taxi went whizzing by. Bennett grabbed my hand to pull me back, without even thinking about it, and all of a sudden, there we were—holding hands right there in the street, where anyone could see us. Just like boyfriend and girlfriend. I felt terrific, like jumping and skipping and running around in circles, like nothing could make my day get any better. But then it did get even better, because Bennett went on holding my hand all the rest of the way home.

As soon as I was back inside the house, I called Liesel. Things had gone better with Bennett than I ever could have expected, so I didn't see any reason to quit while I was ahead. She picked up on the fourth ring.

"Liesel? It's Flan."

"Who?" she shouted.

"Flan Flood!" I yelled back. It sounded like she was in a wind tunnel or something. "I really need to talk to you."

"I'm really rather busy, Flan."

"Please? It's important."

There was a long pause like she didn't know if she wanted to hang up on me or not. But she finally said, "Meet me at Serendipity in half an hour—I don't have time to go all the way downtown!"

And so, five minutes after coming home from

school feeling content and optimistic, I was in a cab on my way to the Upper East Side, feeling worried and nervous again. I just hoped Liesel wouldn't hold a grudge.

Serendipity is one of the cutest places in New York, with Tiffany lamps, pink walls, and little white two-top tables that look like something from a doll's house. The food is even cute, with entrees like the Shake, Batter, and Bowl and the Madame Butterfly, and they sell all kinds of stuff in the front of the store—lunch boxes and windup toys and packages of chocolate—so it almost looks like a toy shop from the street. It's every little girl's favorite restaurant (and probably a lot of little boys' too, even though they'd never admit it).

It's also a great place for celebrity spotting—the last time I was there, Gwyneth Paltrow was eating lunch with her two kids—which is probably how Liesel knew about it in the first place. Also, it's on Sixtieth near Bloomingdale's, her parents' part of town, where the streets are wide and clean, the dogs have beauty shops, and the old women start wearing their fur coats with the first cool breeze of autumn.

As soon as we walked in, I spotted Liesel sitting at a table in the corner, wearing Dolce sunglasses and a dove-gray strapless dress made of some luxurious material. She was talking to the waiter. As soon as she saw me, she waved me over to the table and ordered me a frozen hot chocolate, this really delicious drink they have there. Then she looked across the table intently. Her hair was up in this twist that looked very chic but also kind of severe, and for a second I thought she was about to yell at me. Then she sighed and shook her head.

"Flan, Flan, Flan. What *are* you going to do?" she asked, unfolding her napkin and setting it on her lap.

"I don't know." I looked down at my place mat. "I was hoping that maybe if I talked to you—"

"No, not about me. About Sara-Beth. She's still very upset, you know."

My stomach churned. "I know."

"She trusted you—it's very hard to earn her trust—and you completely let her down." Liesel held up one hand like she was stopping traffic. "I know Sara-Beth can be difficult at times, but she's also very vulnerable. She never had a real childhood, you know. Did you see that piece in the *Times*?"

"Yeah." I looked over at one of the Tiffany lamps. It had stained-glass birds flying across its shade. I wished I could be free like that. "You know, I didn't write those mean things about Sara-Beth—I really didn't. I was writing notes with a couple of friends at school, and—you believe me, don't you?"

Liesel sighed. "Of course I do, Flan. But it's not me you have to convince. You have to show Sara-Beth you're not ashamed of her—that you really think of her as a friend."

I nodded. "Well, I sort of had an idea of how to do it."

So I told her about the party: about how I was inviting Bennett and his friends and Meredith and Judith from school, but also SBB, Liesel, and Philippa—about how I wanted to bring my two worlds together at my house, so everybody—family, friends, whatever—would know how special they were to me. When I was done explaining, Liesel had a dazzling smile on her face. She clasped my hands in hers.

"I should have known you'd come up with the perfect solution. And you're going to throw the most fabulous party. So fabulous, they'll be begging on their hands and knees to keep you in their lives. On their *hands and knees*! And I'm going to plan it for you."

"Oh no, Liesel, you don't have to do that."

"Of course I do! Flan, this is my specialty, my forte, my gift. And you must never let a girl waste her gift." She opened her purse and took out a planner. "It's Saturday, correct?"

"Uh . . . Friday."

"Hmm, I'll have to shuffle some things around. But never mind, that's not important. Who should we get for the entertainment? I have Avril's number in my cell, but you'll want someone classier, I would think. How about Leland Brinker? Or Norah Jones? She still owes me a favor or two—"

"Wait, wait, wait." I thought of Bennett and how embarrassed he'd been about his own small-time party. If he showed up to find Alanis Morissette playing a concert in my backyard, he'd just start feeling awful all over again. Besides, I didn't want to blow everyone away—I just wanted to show them I cared. So I shook my head. "I don't want you to go to all this trouble."

"But it's no trouble! This is what I do."

"No, I know, it's just that . . ." I tried to think how to put this nicely. "Listen, a party's a great idea, but I don't want it to be a big deal. I just want to do something nice and low-key."

Liesel looked confused. She shut her purse with a click. "But Flanny darling, *why*?"

"I dunno, I can't explain it. A party with Norah Jones and a million guests and I dunno, paparazzi, would be cool and everything. It just isn't . . . me."

Liesel bit her perfect mauve lip. I could tell she

thought I was completely crazy, and for a second I thought about taking back what I'd just said. But when I stayed silent, she nodded very slowly.

"All right, fine," she said. "We'll do it your way, then."

I smiled, then squinted past her at a pink-and-blond figure taking a seat at a nearby table. "Oh my God, is that Reese Witherspoon over there?"

Liesel snuck a glance over her shoulder, then snapped her fingers at the waiter and hurriedly dropped some bills on the table. "We need to get out of here, darling. I haven't returned her calls for *months*."

"But—"

Before I could finish, Liesel rushed me out onto the sidewalk, where she shouldered a family of tourists out of the way and strode across the street. As soon as we started walking at a normal pace again, I asked tentatively, "So, do you think you can still help me with the party? Even though I don't want Norah Jones to be there?"

"How can you even ask such a thing? Of course I'll help you, Flan. In fact, I'll consider it a special challenge. Like tightrope walking without a net."

"That's awesome. Thanks so much, Liesel."

"Don't thank me! If anything, I should be thanking you. After all, you did rescue me from the clutches of that vile *artiste*. Thank God he's almost done with the mural now." She sniffed. "Besides, I'd do it anyway. You deserve it. Not everyone can throw a good party, even with my help, but you can. You have that *je ne sais quoi*, you know."

"*Je ne sais* what?"

"Don't tell me you haven't seen it in yourself, snookums, because it's there in spades. You'll go far."

"Huh." I didn't know quite what she meant, but I took it as a compliment. "Thanks, Liesel."

She touched up her lipstick and gave me a smile. "I can't wait to see you shine on Friday night. This party is just the beginning of the beginning—you just wait, darling."

Liesel hailed me a cab, and we air-kissed good-bye. As I rode back through the city, I looked out the windows. Stylish young women walked dogs that matched their purses; cute boys sat on park benches, reading novels or listening to iPods. I saw boutiques and furniture stores and a strange apartment building that looked like a castle, and somehow all of it seemed new and exciting. Maybe Liesel was right—maybe I did have a *je ne sais quoi*. Maybe things really were going to get better, now that I was being myself.

I daydreamed about the party, about how things would suddenly seem simple and laid-back and chill once I had all the important people in my life in the same place at the same time. I pictured Bennett and me lounging around on my living room floor, solving algebra problems together, and I imagined Judith and Meredith and me walking uptown to buy prom dresses. None of it seemed half as impossible as it had that morning, and it was all because I'd reached out to my friends. It occurred to me for the first time in a while that this really was what friends were for—to make people feel good, instead of always just cruddy and stressed out. I started to feel like maybe I was figuring things out—like I had things together.

Chapter 27

I took the cab almost all the way home before I realized I had at least one more stop to make. So instead of going all the way to Perry Street, I had the driver stop at the corner of Washington and Horatio Street. I got out, paid, then started walking.

Philippa also lives in a town house in the West Village, like me, but her street is kind of weird—it's one of those crooked little lanes that sort of loops back on itself, so it wasn't easy to find her place, even though she'd left me her address and directions the day she moved out of my house. Finally, about the third time I walked up and down the street, I found it. It was this prewar building that I guess they'd redone or something, because it was really pretty, with sad-looking stone lions on either side of the front steps and an old-fashioned wood front door that looked like it should be an entrance to the magic land of Narnia.

As I walked up to the door, I thought about Philippa and Mickey. I hoped they'd worked things out. I'd seen them at parties and stuff in the past, when they were happy, and they always seemed like the world's cutest couple to me. Mickey was shorter than Philippa, and sort of round-looking, but he had this contagious sense of humor and craziness to him, and he was always funniest when he was around Philippa, like he was willing to do anything to make her smile. Philippa had more of an intelligent toughness to her, and she tended to be kind of aloof and quiet sometimes. But Mickey brought out a sweeter, more relaxed side of her—maybe because with his clowning around, it's hard for anyone to stay detached. One time, when Patch and Jonathan and I went to a party at a karaoke bar, Mickey ended up belting out this Celine Dion song, "All By Myself," at the top of his lungs, waving his arms at Philippa's table, and even though they were sort of broken up then she'd ended up laughing hysterically and going home with him in a cab.

I wondered if I'd ever have a real, steady boyfriend like that. I found myself thinking of Bennett again. But by now I was at Philippa's door, so bracing myself, I took a deep breath and rang the bell. I hoped she wouldn't still be totally furious at me, but I was ready for whatever might happen.

After a long time, I was about to ring the bell again when the door finally swung open. There was Philippa, looking all disheveled and out of breath, wearing a boy's T-shirt and a pair of cut-off shorts.

"Flan! Thank God it's you. I was scared my dad was home early," she said, leading me into the house. "Hang on a sec. Mickey's hiding under my bed." She ran halfway up the stairs, yelling, "Mickey! Mickey, you can come down now!"

"Sorry if I'm interrupting something," I said, feeling way awkward all of a sudden.

"No, don't worry about it." She glanced over her shoulder and added a little doubtfully, "I'm glad to see you." She came back down the stairs and flopped into one of the chairs in the living room. "How've you been?"

I decided to cut right to the point. "I feel terrible about what happened with you guys the last time I saw you. Seriously. I hope you don't hate me."

"Jesus, Flan, I couldn't hate you." Philippa smiled and shook her head. "I think I was just pissed that night because there was this big scene between Mickey and Sara-Beth and he ended up skipping out on me again. But we've made up now. Anyway, it's not me you have to apologize to. It's Sara-Beth."

I nodded. "I know. I'm throwing a party at my house

to try to make up with everybody. That guy I like's going to be there—so are my friends from school. Do you think she'll come?"

Philippa squinted, thinking. "Have you talked to her yet?"

"Well, I've left her a couple of voice mails, but she hasn't called me back."

I glanced around the room. The house was decorated the way I imagined an art dealer's would be: in neutral colors, mostly white and tan, so the art stood out that much more. There were paintings and drawings hanging all over the walls—I saw one with flying goats and people playing musical instruments that looked like it was by Marc Chagall, who I studied last year in art history—and there were little marble pillars around the room, with sculptures on them that were lit up with spotlights like in a museum.

"The thing is, she's mad, but I think she wants to make up with you." Philippa smiled. "Nobody can stay mad forever. Mickey and I fight every second day, but I'm starting to think it keeps things interesting."

Just then, Mickey came jumping down the stairs. He had a little patchy beard that somehow made him look both older and sillier at the same time.

"Hey, Flan," he said, ruffling my hair like I was still a little kid. He tried to climb into the chair with

Philippa, but she hit him with a pillow. He made a roaring sound and grabbed her. Then they started tickling each other, until finally they were both sitting in the chair, with Philippa on his lap. With some couples, stuff like that would make me feel really left out, but it was sweet to see them together like that. They were so much in love that it kind of wore off on me.

"So what can we do for you?" he asked once we'd all stopped laughing.

"I was just coming by to invite you guys to my party. It's not going to be a lot of people or anything, but it should be fun." I handed them the invitations. "It's on Friday. All the information's in there."

"A party? At the Floods'? I'm so there," Mickey said, ripping open his invitation. "It's been all summer since you guys threw the last one."

"But wait a sec. Friday?" Philippa turned to Mickey. "Isn't that the day your friend's doing that skate-boarding thing? That competition?"

"Oh, shoot. You're right, babe."

"Maybe we can come over after," Philippa said to me. "It's just that this has been planned for weeks and weeks. Mickey's friend Jorge is supposed to be doing this half-pipe thing, and we promised him we'd go even before we broke up and got back together again."

I tried not to look disappointed. "Well, my party's not going to go that late anyway. But if you get a chance, come on over."

Philippa nodded. "I really want to. Especially because I'd like to meet this famous Bennett."

I blushed. "Well, that's no big deal."

"No big deal? Of course it is! You're my friend and this is your love life! What do friends do but meddle in each other's love lives?" She leaned forward. "So how can I meddle? Do you need any advice?"

"Sure. Just tell me how you got into such a good relationship."

Philippa smacked the side of Mickey's head. "You hear that, Romeo? She thinks we have a good relationship."

Mickey blinked, acting astonished. "Have I entered a parallel universe?"

"Oh, stop it, you guys," I said, laughing. "You know you're great."

"The greatness goes in and out." Philippa lay back in Mickey's arms like she was swooning. "That's why we have to keep dumping each other."

"And making out with other girls," added Mickey, deadpan. "No, wait, only Philippa does that."

"Don't try my patience. I might switch back." Philippa kissed him to show she was just kidding, then turned back to me. "Listen, the best advice I can give you is: show him who you really are. Don't pretend to be someone else just so he'll like you."

"Yeah," I agreed. "You're totally right. Even if I did take forever to figure that out."

Philippa shrugged. "We're all learning. It's hard to get close to someone, you know? Unless their backyard connects to yours and they come over to bother you every five minutes."

"Hey!" Mickey protested. We all laughed.

I hung out for a few more minutes and had a soda, then walked back to my house. It was so great how Philippa and Mickey were completely comfortable together—like they'd found everything they always wanted wrapped up in the other person and now they didn't have to keep looking anymore. I wondered if I'd feel that way about Bennett as I got to know him better—or if he'd start to feel that way about me.

Chapter 28

Philippa or no Philippa, I really was going to have a party on Friday. Now the only thing left was to make sure it was okay with my parents. To make sure there were no snags, I just did what Patch and February taught me to a long time ago: I asked my mom when my dad was out of the house. He stepped out for a bagel about five minutes before I left for school, so the timing was perfect. I found my mom arranging flowers in the living room, and I don't think she was really listening when I asked her, because she just sang out, "That sounds great, Flan! Charge it," like she always does when I'm asking for new jeans or whatever. But this time I didn't just want money.

"Listen, Mom. I want you and Dad to be around for it too. And Patch. And Feb, if anyone ever hears from her again."

"Honey, that's so sweet." She smiled. "It'll be so nice to meet all your friends."

I grinned and went to call Liesel. We had things to do.

Planning a party sounds like it would be easy, especially when the party's only for thirteen people— or, in this case, eleven, since Philippa and Mickey had already flaked out on me by the time I started buying stuff and making arrangements. But actually, party planning takes a lot of thought. You can't just blow up some balloons and order a clown, not when you're fourteen years old and trying to get all the crazy pieces of your too-complicated life together in one place. So over the next couple of days, I pretty much focused on getting everything exactly the way I wanted it.

First there was the question, Where's the party going to be, exactly? In our house, the answer's pretty simple: It has to be in the living room/kitchen area. I guess I could have had it in the attic, but then I'd have to move all of Feb's dusty purses and old Barneys boxes out of the way; plus, I'd have the additional problem of carrying all the food and drinks up two flights of stairs every single time. Then there was the basement, but that was pretty much out, in my opinion anyway. It's mostly unfinished concrete down there, except for one part of the space that's carpeted with Astroturf from some brief period right after we moved in, when Patch thought he wanted to be a baseball player. Fake grass, uncovered swinging light-bulbs, and windowless subterranean concrete walls were definitely not the look I was going for.

So it had to be the living room. Which meant that, in order for the party to feel like it really was my party, and not just some sort of less-wild rehash of one of my brother's, I had some redecorating to do.

Liesel helped a lot. She and I agreed that the lighting for my party should be less bright than daytime and less tacky than the flashing disco lamps left over from my sister's after-prom. So we went to this insane lamp store on the Lower East Side, where they have every kind of lamp known to man, and wandered around looking at lamps for like two hours. It was hard, because we had to find something that was awesome but that didn't look like I was so spoiled that I could afford to buy whatever I want, because we both agreed that'd look gross. I finally decided on these sort of Japanese lantern-looking things. They were like yellow paper tubes that lit up from the inside, and once we had them plugged in, I could see they were just perfect—not too bright, but not too dark either. It was kind of like candlelight during an evening thunderstorm.

So then there was the food, and drinks. My brother and sister let me have beers sometimes, and I think my parents know that, but it's sort of an unspoken rule in our family that none of us drink around my parents. Besides, I didn't really want to have alcohol at my party anyway—I don't like the way it tastes much, and I was pretty sure that Judith, Meredith, and Bennett hadn't really had any experience drinking, which meant that it would probably have a weird effect on them. And weirdness, especially drunken weirdness, was definitely not something I wanted to have at my party.

So I decided that we'd just have Shirley Temples and Roy Rogers, plus hummus and pita bread and red velvet cupcakes from my favorite bakery. On the day of the party, I also planned to cut up a bunch of fruit and put it in one of those bowls made from half a scooped-out watermelon, which was kind of ambitious since I'd never done anything like that before, but I was determined. Plus we'd have a cheese plate, with crackers, and some little tiny sandwiches like you can get at Tea for Two. Of course, we'd also have to have mineral water and sesame crunch candies in a special dish for SBB.

Because I still hoped she was coming, even though I still hadn't been able to get her on the phone. The first few times I called, I think she just didn't want to talk to me, because I went straight through to her voice mail, but after that it was like her cell phone had gotten disconnected or something, which made me worry. And I had no idea where she was living, so I couldn't hand-deliver the invitation.

I felt a little sick every time I thought about how things had ended between us. But I'd told both Liesel and Philippa to invite SBB to the party on my behalf, so I hoped she'd get the news through them and start to understand how sorry I was.

But at least my other friends seemed to have forgiven me. That week, I hung out with Meredith, Judith, and Bennett every lunchtime and a couple of days after school. And whenever I wasn't hanging out with friends or planning for the party, I had a ton of homework to keep me distracted from thinking too much about SBB. I know this sounds kind of weird, but I even found myself getting interested in my classes. In English class, for example, we read this Fitzgerald story called "Bernice Bobs Her Hair," and even though it was set way back in the twenties, there was something about it that I felt like I really got. That girl Bernice seemed like a real person to me—I wouldn't want to cut off all my hair either. And the way the parties were described I could totally picture them, even though at our parties now you're lucky if you can get just one guy to dance with you, let alone a whole bunch, one after the other.

I doubted there would be any dancing at my party, but I still wanted to have music. So in the evenings I started making a mix CD of a bunch of my favorite songs, which I planned to have on in the background while we sat around talking and stuff. I'd never made a mix CD for myself before, and it surprised me how fun it was. With each song I chose, I got a new chance to show my friends who I was and what I was like. It was great. I've never been at a party where I really liked all the music before, but this was my night and I was going to do things my way.

Friday, the day of the party, I rushed home from school to get everything in place, even though people weren't supposed to start coming over till seven-thirty. On the way home I picked up the red velvet cupcakes from the bakery, and the whole time I was waiting in line I kept looking at the clock every two seconds. As soon as I had the cupcakes, I practically ran the rest of the way home. The minute I walked in the door, I set up the lamps and put a tablecloth on the coffee table. I put hummus and pita bread on a glass dish, arranged the cupcakes on a tray, and made a pitcher of Shirley Temples and a pitcher of Roy

Rogers. Then I was basically done, and it was only four-thirty. I felt nervous and excited and like anything might happen, so I decided to work on decorating a little more just to keep myself busy. My mom walked in the door just as I was getting up on a chair to hang some red crepe paper from the ceiling.

"Flanny, sweetie, what are you doing?" she asked, setting down her tennis racket and her yellow gym bag. "Get down from that chair—you'll hurt yourself."

I ripped down the crepe paper and climbed down off the chair. It looked stupid anyway. "I'm setting up for my party, remember?"

"Is that today? But your father and I wanted to be here for it."

"I thought you were going to be."

"No, tonight's the benefit dinner for—oh, some sort of medical association. You should ask your father; I never remember these things."

"What?" This was the first I'd ever heard about it. I tried to stop myself from feeling annoyed, but it was hard. After all, how hard is it to remember your youngest kid's first high school party? It doesn't happen every day. "But Mom, how's this going to work? I have people coming over. Don't you and Dad need to be around here? To supervise or whatever?"

"Aren't you a little too old for that?"

I knew that most kids would kill for their parents to act like this—but as I'd been finding out over the last several weeks, I wasn't like most kids. I was Flan Flood, and for once in my life I just wanted a sane, normal party. "No."

"Hmm." She scrunched up her forehead and touched one finger to her lips; whenever she does that she reminds me so much of Marian the Librarian from *The Music Man* that I have to smile. "I know. We'll call your brother. He can keep an eye on things and make sure they don't get out of hand."

Patch Flood *supervising* a party? I tried not to laugh. "Where is he anyway? I haven't seen him since . . . day before yesterday, I think."

"Apparently he's been staying with some friends. Your father called his cell this morning and someone answered and said everything was fine."

"Who was it?"

"Could her name have been Veronique? I'm not sure—I'll call now, and if she answers, I'll demand to speak to my son." Then she started laughing, as if acting like a real mom were the funniest thing in the world.

I shook my head and flopped down on the couch while my mom went to the kitchen. From where I was sitting I could hear her dialing, then talking to Patch.

"Patch? Yes, actually, we do need you here. . . . Oh no, nothing like that. Your sister is having some friends over—yes, I know. . . . No, the man from the surfboard shop left a message—he said it wouldn't be ready for another week. Now, sweetie, Flan is having some friends over—I told you about it the other day. I was just wondering if you could come home and keep an eye on things. . . . I certainly hope it's over by two o'clock! All right . . . Yes. Your father and I might see you when we get in tonight. . . . Well, tell her we say hello too." She hung up. "He should be here around eight."

"But my party starts at seven-thirty!"

"You'll just have to behave yourselves for half an hour, then," she said, shaking her head like she does when she finds something funny. I sighed, but even I had to admit this conversation *was* kind of silly. It wasn't like I'd never been home alone before.

All of a sudden, I heard a ferocious sound—like a wolf chowing down on an entire pasture of sheep. I sat straight up, and there was Noodles, tearing into the pita bread like he was starving.

"Bad dog! Bad! Bad!"

Noodles cowered, pressing his ears flat back on his head like he was incredibly sorry, but he didn't have me fooled. He was still chewing.

"This dog is new," my mom said. She stared down at him. His eyes went wide as he looked back up at her. And then he ran out of the room and up the stairs. "Do you walk him?"

"Yes! Every morning before school and then . . . other times too. Is it okay if I keep him?"

"Darling, of course. Don't ask such silly questions."

So while my mom went upstairs to shower and get dressed for the benefit dinner—she was meeting my dad somewhere downtown in about an hour—I put my shoes back on and, with Noodles in tow, walked to the grocery store to buy some more pita bread. Last-minute disasters—what would my life be without them?

I was trying to stop Noodles from peeing on a blue motor scooter that someone had parked on the sidewalk, when my cell phone rang. Still pulling on the leash with one hand, I reached into my pocket with the other, pulled out the phone, and flipped it open. The number was Liesel's.

"Hey," I said, practically dragging Noodles down the street. He found a half-eaten falafel on the sidewalk and, even though it was covered with tread marks, pounced on it hungrily. I loved the little guy, but sometimes his eating habits were just gross. Then again, maybe it's my fault for feeding him human food so often. "Drop that, Noodles! Drop it! Sorry, Liesel. What's up?"

"Flan, darling, I have the most horrendous news. I'm not going to be able to come to your party."

"What?" I was so surprised, I almost dropped the

leash. "But we've been planning it together, like, all week!"

"I know, I know, and I feel absolutely miserable about the whole thing." She sighed deeply. "I just don't see how it can be helped. You see, they need me at Cube tonight. The reviewer from *Time Out* is coming, and if he finds anyone tacky or uncouth, the write-up will be terrible."

"But what am I supposed to do? How can I make my party cool without you there?"

"I don't know, snookums. It's a catastrophe."

"This sucks so much. First Philippa can't come—then my parents forget about the whole thing—and now you're not going to be there either."

"Your parents won't be there?"

"No! They forgot all about it and made other plans. They're sending Patch in to supervise. Isn't that insane?"

Liesel laughed, and even from across town I could practically see her eyes sparkling.

"Darling, why didn't you tell me? If Patch is the chaperone, you'll have no trouble making the party unforgettable. Ciao for now. I'll text later to see how you're holding up." She hung up.

I stopped walking and looked down at my cell phone in disgust. Unbelievable. For a minute I started to get really mad at Liesel—I'd counted on her to be there, to help keep the party under control. How could she cancel on me at the last minute? I made myself take a deep breath and concentrated on getting to the grocery store in one piece. After all, it was still my party. Even if things weren't working out exactly the way I'd planned, I was still in charge. Maybe with a little luck I'd be able to turn things around.

You're not really supposed to bring pets into the grocery store, but Noodles is so cute that no one seemed to care. I picked up the hummus and pita bread and carried them up to the cash register, still thinking. Maybe in a way it was a good thing that Liesel wasn't there. She was a party expert, sure, but not a party expert for fourteen-year-olds, and she'd probably have been bored out of her mind anyway. And when she gets bored, she can kind of have a catty streak. Still, I'd rather have my friends there, even with all their flaws. This day had gone from bad to worse

When I went back outside I flipped open my cell phone again and tried calling Sara-Beth one last time. But yet again, she didn't answer. And then all of a sudden I felt as crappy as I ever have in my life.

The rest of the way home, I worried about the party. I had invited ten people: Bennett, Judith, Meredith, Liesel, Sara-Beth, Philippa, Mickey, Jules, and Eric. Plus Patch and Feb. And me. And already I knew at least three of them weren't going to make it. Even my parents had canceled on me. I hadn't wanted it to be huge, but this was getting ridiculous.

It reminded me of this one time back in third grade, when Olivia, a friend from Miss Mallard's, threw a birthday party at her house. Olivia was kind of nerdy back then, always wearing maroon turtlenecks and stuff, and she didn't have a lot of friends, but still, when she invited every girl in our class she kind of expected at least half of them to show up. On the day of the party, though, it ended up being just her, me, and this overpriced Russian magician that her parents had hired from some sort of crazy European birthday party service. He pulled about twenty dollars' worth of quarters out of my ear, then asked for them all back. It was the lamest party of all time, and Olivia and I never talked about it ever again. No way did I want tonight to turn out like that.

When I got home, though, I started to feel a little better. The living room looked really nice the way that I'd decorated it—just the Japanese-looking lamps made a huge difference—and I told myself I was making way too big a deal about this whole thing. People would either like me, or they wouldn't. If I had to throw the best party of all time to win their friendship, then they probably weren't worth hanging out with anyway. So after setting up the hummus and stuff, I made myself stop obsessing over the party space.

I fed Noodles, changed into this really cute green Miu Miu dress I'd bought when Liesel and I went shopping together, then curled up in a chair with a book to wait for my guests. I was kidding myself if I thought I could get through even one page, though, because I couldn't concentrate at all. Mostly I just kept reading the same paragraph over and over until I finally shut the book. I looked out the window. I could tell it was really fall now, because it was getting dark earlier. By seven-thirty, it was almost like night outside.

Patch showed up first—actually on time, if you can believe that.

"I'm so glad to see you," I said, leading him into the living room. "All these people canceled on me—and I can't believe Mom and Dad aren't going to be here. So, does it look okay? What do you think?"

Patch laughed at me. "You're worrying way too much."

"Maybe you're right." I threw myself down into a chair and sighed. "Patch, how come you're so laid-back?"

My brother shrugged. "Things have a way of working themselves out, you know? Just take a breath."

"Yeah, you're right." I put my feet up on an ottoman and took some deep, relaxing breaths. But then the doorbell rang again, and I jumped right back up. I could relax later. Right now, the real guests were starting to arrive.

The minute I saw Meredith and Judith, I was glad I'd dressed up. Meredith was wearing this cute lacy dress that looked like it was from the sixties, and her hair was down all the way, with these awesome barrettes in it that had artificial flowers glued to them. Judith had on a halter top and heels. And, even though it wasn't my birthday, they'd brought gifts. Judith was carrying a bottle of sparkling cider, and Meredith had made me a belt out of bottle caps. It sounds like it would be ugly, I know, but it was actually cool. Even if it had been the tackiest thing ever, though, I wouldn't have cared. It was just amazing that they'd put so much effort into getting ready for my party. Obviously this was a bigger deal to them than I'd realized.

"Wow, this is so nice," I said, taking the presents. "You guys really didn't have to do this."

"We just felt bad we doubted you and everything,"

said Meredith shyly, tucking her hair behind her ears.

"Oh." I felt really touched, almost like I was going to start crying. "Well, you guys had every right to doubt me. I'm sorry I kept so many secrets. From now on, I won't. It was really stupid."

"We were the stupid ones," Judith admitted. "Or really, I was. Meredith kept telling me we could trust you, but I guess I just didn't believe her."

"Well, it doesn't matter," I said. "Come on in." I stepped out of the doorway so they could come inside. Judith handed me the bottle of cider, but Meredith held on to the bottle-cap belt, turning it over in her hands like she was worried I wouldn't like it or something.

"Let me show you how it works," she said.

She was still showing me how the buckle she'd made fastened—it was adjustable, and kind of complicated—as we walked into the living room. I glanced around in surprise. Patch was gone—it was like he'd evaporated or something.

But before I could say anything about it, Meredith and Judith had started wandering around the living room, looking sort of confused. And in a flash, I could tell just what they were thinking: Where were my other friends? My family? My scene? They cooed over the refreshments and the cool sofa and every-thing, but I could tell that they thought I was still hiding something from them.

"Hey, I know this isn't what you were expecting," I said, standing awkwardly in a corner of the room.

Meredith bit her lip. "Well, it is a little . . . quieter."

"Yeah, I know. When you hear about the Flood house, people are always talking about our parties and how it's a huge hangout. But the thing is, it's this way a lot of the time too. My parents travel a lot, and when my brother and sister are out having their adventures, I'm actually just alone."

Judith frowned. "That must be so weird. I'm sorry, Flan."

At first I was afraid she was being sarcastic; it took me a second to realize she was actually sympathizing with me. But before things got too heavy, Noodles ran in, wagging his tail and squealing, and Meredith and Judith practically went into hysterics.

"Oh, he's so cute," shrieked Meredith. Noodles stood on his hind legs, waving his front paws at her, until she got down on the ground and held him in her lap.

"How old is he?" asked Judith, scratching him behind the ears.

I shrugged. "I don't really know."

"So he's a rescue, then?"

I thought of the tacky model from the bar—her Mickey Mouse shirt, her belly button ring, her flip-flops.

"You could say that, yeah," I answered.

"Well, he is amazing," Judith said. "He's the cutest little thing I've ever seen!" Noodles promptly licked her face—I think he knows when he's being compli-mented.

We sat around, eating red velvet cupcakes and listening to the party CD I'd made. Meredith recom-mended some bands to me and promised to burn me copies of their albums. We mostly just joked around and gossiped about people from school until the guys showed up.

The second the doorbell rang, all three of us leapt up. And even though it made them look kind of over-eager, Judith and Meredith came with me, giggling and fixing their hair, when I got up to answer it.

Bennett, Eric, and Jules were standing on the steps, looking awkward as I swung the door open. Bennett was wearing a collared Madras shirt and he had his hair slicked back. He smiled at me, sort of shyly but with his dimples showing, and held out a bunch of yellow lilies. How did he know they're my favorite?

"These are for you," he said. He quickly added,

"From all of us," but before he could get the words out, Meredith and Judith went, "Awww . . ."

"Thanks so much," I said, grinning.

Bennett blushed. I think that if other people in our class at school could've seen him right then, they never would have called him the *second*-cutest boy in tenth grade. Especially because Eric, who was supposedly the first, was standing right next to him in wrinkled blue jeans, with this big scowl on his face like he was too cool to be there or something. It was definitely not the kind of expression you see on male models, that's for sure. Even Jules looked cuter, because at least he was smiling. He stood behind the other two, wearing this vintage suit jacket that looked like it was from the seventies or something, and *he* looked like he couldn't have been happier. The minute she saw him, Meredith looked away and stared straight down at her feet—I think she was glad he'd shown up too.

"It's so great to see you guys," I said, stepping aside to let them in. "I'm so glad you could come."

"So this is the famous Flood house," said Eric, striding into the living room before anyone else. He looked around and sniffed the air. "Hmm. Hmmm. Not too shabby. Yeah, it's all right, Flan. I'm glad to finally see it myself. You know, your brother's got a rep for being the biggest party animal in the West Village. But don't worry, I never really bought it."

"Thanks," I said, rolling my eyes. I went out to the kitchen to put the flowers in some water. As I was running the tap, it occurred to me for the first time that maybe Eric was jealous of my brother. And now they were both here. Oh boy, oh boy. This was going to be some evening.

I went back out to the living room, where my friends were all drinking the sparkling cider Judith had brought. I sat down next to Bennett on the sofa and poured myself a glass. The guys were trying to make conversation with Judith and Meredith, but it wasn't going too well.

"So, Judith, who do you have for history class?"

Giggle, giggle.

"Hey, Meredith, you know this song?"

Shy silence.

After a while, Jules and Bennett were actually able to get a conversation going about movies—Meredith mumbled that she liked pirates, and Judith giggled something about flying snakes—but they didn't have much help from Eric, who was sitting in one of the chairs with his arms crossed, still scowling. I wondered how they'd managed to drag him there. Probably he'd just wanted to see our house himself so he could go back to school and say parties at the Flood house weren't all that.

Finally we poured out the rest of the cider, and the party fell into a real lull.

"I have some board games up in my room," I offered. "We could play Scrabble—or Monopoly."

"I call the race car," Bennett volunteered.

"I know a better game we could play," suggested Jules. He had a kind of mischievous grin on his face and even before he reached for the cider bottle, I knew what he had in mind.

"Oh no, not spin-the-bottle!" cried Judith, delighted. "Let me go first."

She jumped up out of her chair and went to the coffee table.

"Wait a second, we have to sit in a circle," said Jules.

So we all sat down on the carpet in a circle around the table. I moved the box of red velvet cupcakes (which were now half gone) down onto the floor, and Judith gave the bottle a spin, then squealed. Because it ended up pointing right . . . at . . . Eric.

There was a long, really awkward moment as Eric stared at her like she was a total stranger on the subway, and then I realized that Eric was actually nervous about this kiss.

"Relax," Bennett said. "It's just a kiss."

"Shut it," Eric said. And everybody sort of giggled.

"If you don't want to . . ." Judith said.

"Of course I want to!" Eric said, and then his face got this look that was sort of like, "Okay, I'll do this, but I am really, really embarrassed." He closed his eyes, puckered up, and leaned slowly over the coffee table. But just as she moved her face close to his—

"Oh my God, it's Patch Flood!" Judith shrieked. Meredith, bringing a cup of cider to her lips, promptly dropped it into her lap.

I turned to look, and there he was: my brother, standing in the doorway to the kitchen, wearing his board shorts and a clean T-shirt. His hair was all sunbleached and wavy. And he was holding a bag of chocolate animals from Li-Lac, my favorite candy store.

"Hey," he said with an effortless smile. "I realized I hadn't brought anything for the party, so I snuck out the back door. Hope you like these—Flan always used to have them at her parties when she was a little girl."

Judith and Meredith stared at each other, their mouths still hanging open. Eric crumpled up his napkin and threw it over his shoulder in disgust since he'd been totally called out as somebody who had never really kissed a girl before, even though he was handsome. If he'd been jealous of Patch before, he was crazy with anger and embarrassment now. Finally, Meredith was the first one to speak: "Flan," she whispered, "this is the best party ever!"

I was glad she thought so. And it was pretty much the most perfect evening. Except for one still-missing invitee.

Chapter 31

"This is a really great party," Bennett said. We'd gone outside to get a moment to ourselves before he had to go. He ran his hand through his hair self-consciously. "I really hate that I'm going to have to go soon. But like I said, my brother's getting home from college for the weekend, and—"

"Say no more," I told him. "I totally understand."

"Yeah, well, you'll have to tell me how the Clue game turns out. I still think Professor Plum was involved somehow."

I laughed. "I'll tell you all about it in school on Monday."

"Actually, would you like to get together before then? Tomorrow night, maybe? There's this movie playing at the Angelika—"

"Bennett Keating, are you asking me out on a date?"

"Yeah, I guess I am." He rubbed one toe into the step, and I thought about how it made him even cuter that he was so shy. "I mean, if you'd rather not—"

I took his hand. "No. I would absolutely love to."

"Great!" Bennett smiled. I was liking his dimples more all the time. "I'll come by around seven to pick you up."

"Maybe my parents'll actually be around this time. I'm sure they'd like to meet you. They are real, I swear."

"I believe it." Bennett looked at his watch. "Okay, now I really do have to go."

"Sure."

Bennett reached out like he was just going to give me a hug, and I stepped forward to hug him back. But then, at the last second before he let go, he turned his face toward mine—and we kissed. It wasn't on the ear—it wasn't a part of spin-the-bottle—it was a nice, normal kiss, like real couples share, and it was absolutely wonderful. Bennett let go and we stood there for a minute, grinning at each other like idiots.

Then Sara-Beth Benny leapt out from the bushes and totally ruined the moment.

"Oh my God, Flan, is this him?" she shrieked in a stage whisper behind her hand. "The ear man? I'm so glad to see things worked out—finally!"

Bennett turned beet-red, and I think I did too. But at that point, Sara-Beth could've said anything and I wouldn't have gotten mad, I was so glad to see her. Before she could move an inch, I wrapped her in a big hug.

"Sara-Beth! I'm so glad you're here."

She hugged me back and gave me a big smile. "I couldn't stay mad at you for long, Flan. When Philippa told me you wanted me here, I couldn't say no."

"I just feel so bad about what happened. You have no idea."

"If anyone should feel bad, it's me—showing up here looking like this. Ew! I'm a mess!"

Sara-Beth was wearing this little pleated Prada skirt and top, but she had leaves stuck to her back and dirt on her knees. As she started brushing herself off, I wondered how long she'd been hiding there—and why.

"I was about to come in to see your lovely party," she went on, as if answering my question, "when you two came out and I dove into the bushes. That was one thing I learned from the jujitsu course—reflexes!"

"I'm sorry, I don't think we've met," said Bennett, finally bouncing back from his embarrassment. I was glad to see that he was smiling again—it *was* sort

225

of a funny situation if you looked at it right. "I'm Bennett."

"And I'm Sara-Beth Benny," she said, offering her hand like she expected him to kiss it or something.

"Wait a second. I thought you looked familiar, but . . . *the* Sara-Beth Benny?"

"The one and only," I said, and Sara-Beth tossed her hair like the movie star she was.

"Well, it was great to meet you, Sara-Beth," said Bennett. "But I've got to get going. See you tomorrow, Flan." He gave me a long, soulful look in the eyes, like he could barely stand to leave, and squeezed my hand. Then took off down the front steps. He waved just before disappearing down the sidewalk, back toward his apartment building.

"You have no idea how glad I am you're here," I said to Sara-Beth. "You have to believe me—I didn't write those mean things about you."

"Oh, in my heart, I knew that all along. You don't have that kind of meanness in you, Flan. Besides, the handwriting didn't match."

"Match what?"

"Your diary," she said matter-of-factly. "I found it in the desk drawer the first day I was staying with you, when I was looking for the clothespins."

I sighed and shook my head. A few weeks ago, I

would've been mad, or at least freaked out—but now I knew there was nothing written in there that I wouldn't have told her anyway. She might be a little nuts, but I was quickly realizing that she was also my best friend. "Listen, where've you been? I've been trying to call you all day. For a few days, actually. It was like you fell off the face of the earth or something."

"I'd say I was a little closer than that—I was moving into my new house, silly!"

"New house?"

Sara-Beth smacked me playfully, like I should know already. But before I could ask her what in the world she was talking about, she was opening the door and going into my party.

Jules, Eric, Meredith, and Judith were all still playing Clue together, and I heard dice hit the table in a clatter as they all turned in unison to stare at the movie star who'd just burst through the door. Sara-Beth removed her sunglasses with a flourish.

"Sara-Beth Benny," she said to the room. "Pleased to make your acquaintance."

Meredith and Judith looked at each other and screamed, *"Sara-Beth Benny?"*

"I'm so sorry I'm late." Sara-Beth glided across the room. She suddenly seemed so easygoing and social that even I couldn't imagine her crouching behind the sofa, clutching an air horn and wearing my pajama pants. "Do you mind if I jump into the game?" She perched on the arm of Eric's chair, and he stared up at her without blinking, like she was an angel or a vision or something. "How do you play?"

Meanwhile, Meredith and Judith were completely speechless. If they'd been thrilled to meet my brother, they were ecstatic now. With their mouths open and their eyes bugged out, they might as well have been a pair of goldfish.

"How do you know Flan?" asked Jules, the only one in the room—other than me, of course—who wasn't in immediate danger of swooning.

"Oh, we've been friends for ages," said Sara-Beth. "But now, I guess you could say we're neighbors."

"Neighbors?" I asked. I wondered if she was still planning to hide out in one of my closets.

"I just finished moving into the town house right across the street. Isn't that fabulous? It'll be just like you said: we'll have a little bit of space, but we'll still get to spend oodles of time together! In fact, I plan to be over here every afternoon after school. Won't it be wonderful, Flan? You'll do your homework—I'll learn my lines. We'll be bona fide best friends!"

Meredith and Judith both let out delighted little gasps, but I just shook my head and laughed. My life was doomed to be crazy—I knew that now. But it was okay, because I also knew that was just the way I liked it.

The life of an Inside Girl is anything but ordinary.

Find out what happens next in *The Sweetest Thing,* an Inside Girl novel by J. Minter

Flan Flood finally has her life in order. Her new, normal friends from school get along with her celebrity starlet friends, and she couldn't be happier being Just Flan.

But as life is settling down, Flan's friends Judith and Meredith fall for the same guy: hot quarterback Adam, whose smile is as winning as his throwing arm. And when Flan's BFF, teen-starlet Sara-Beth Benny, decides to throw a Halloween party, both of Flan's friends vow to kiss their football prince by midnight at the big bash.

Suddenly, Flan finds herself in the middle of an all-out battle for Adam's attention. Can Flan convince Meredith and Judith that girlfriends are way more important than any guy, or will Flan find herself dangerously stuck in the middle?

"I wish I'd known Flan Flood in high school—and not just because she has a hot older brother with hot older friends (although that totally helps). Don't let the name fool you—this is one girl you must get to know, now."
—Lisi Harrison, author of The Clique

Learn more about Flan and the Inside Girls at www.insidegirlbooks.com

Find out how it all began in the Insiders series, also by J. Minter

"The Insiders are *the* guys to watch. But if you fall in love with them, get in line, right behind ME!"
—Zoey Dean, author of *The A-List*

For more info on the guys, visit
www.insidersbook.com

Wish you could choose a boyfriend as cute as Flan's?

Check out the new series
date him or dump him?
from Bloomsbury

REMEMBER: With more than twenty possible endings in each book, if he's not the boy of your dreams, you can always go back and choose another one!

The Campfire Crush

This summer, you're finally a junior counselor at Camp Butterfield! Do you pair up with your crush for lifeguard training, or flirt with another counselor on a white-water rafting trip?

NOW AVAILABLE

The Dance Dilemma

The junior homecoming dance is right around the corner. Do you join the decorating committee to meet some potential dates, or hit the mall in search of the perfect dress?

AVAILABLE AUGUST 2007

And look for
Date Him or Dump Him? Ski Trip Trouble
coming in Fall 2007!